The Buddhas of Borneo

by

Stuart Ayris

Beaten Track
www.beatentrackpublishing.com

The Buddhas of Borneo

First published (paperback) 2013 by Beaten Track Publishing
Copyright © 2013 Stuart Ayris

All rights reserved.
No part of this publication may be reproduced, stored in a retrieval system, or transmitted, in any form or by any means, without the prior permission of the publisher, nor be otherwise circulated without the publisher's prior consent in any form of binding or cover other than that in which it is published and without a similar condition including this condition being imposed on the subsequent publisher.

The moral right of the author has been asserted.

A CIP catalogue record for this book
is available from the British Library.

ISBN: 978 1 909192 46 1

Cover by Katie W Stewart

Beaten Track Publishing,
Burscough. Lancashire.
www.beatentrackpublishing.com

Contents

Prologue 1
1. Borneo Bound and Yearning...3
2. Leave the Smeary Smoke to those that would Inhale 13
3. This Gorgeous Wild Madness..23
4. Western Shackles 33
5. Shopping Knee and Majesty 43
6. Cavernblack Giggleslip..57
7. Bread on the Water Now 69
8. Smoking a Pipe in the Rain 81
9. Play and Munch..93
10. Starlove..103
Other Books by Stuart Ayris 115

Dedicated to
Frank and Wendy Morrissey

This is a work of fiction.
Names, characters, brands, media and incidents are either the product of the author's imagination or are used fictitiously.

Prologue

The Foreign and Commonwealth Office (FCO) advise against all but essential travel to the coastal area of Sabah running from Kota Kinabatangan Besar (located some 80km south of Sandakan) through to the town of Kunak, and also to the area east of a line running due south from Kunak to the coast. This area includes the town and airport of Lahad Datu, the town of Semporna and the islands in the immediate vicinity.

If you're travelling to other parts of eastern Sabah (e.g. Tawau, Sandakan, Sepilok or the Danum Valley) you should exercise a high degree of caution, keep up to date with developments, and follow the advice of your tour operator and the local authorities.

There is a general threat from terrorism. Foreign nationals have been kidnapped in East Malaysia and this threat remains, particularly in the islands off eastern Sabah.

Malaysia is a multicultural, but mostly Muslim country.

1. Borneo Bound and Yearning

...like a diamond sutra in the sky.
Loosen up Lucy for we're off the ground and the only sound is the sound of the ground wafting us up into the universe blue.
...in the air, in the air, in the air, in the air
that's
where
you'll
find
me.

Don't mind me. I'll be fine and toppering don't you know? I'm leaving Tollesbury for Borneo. But that's OK. It's all heaven to me.

Spangle you hidden stars and spangle good. One sweet day I'll treat you to a pint of cheap red wine with ice cubes and you'll see that we all sparkle, sparkle in the universe blue.

...in the air, in the air, in the air, in the air.

Strangers to the right of me, strangers to the front of me. Stuck in the middle without you. I've got a window seat and the finest view in the bigbird house. All buckled up for the ride confined in tonnes of steel and at the mercy of conscious pilot. Choose well, good sir, choose well. Just remember that I'm Brian and so's my wife. Then you'll be just doody dandy. I'd raise a glass to you right now but aghast I realise this is a dry flight. Brunei Airlines. Dry flight. What was I thinking? Air hostesses all red lipstick openmouthed stunning magnificence. But still. Dry flight. What was I thinking?

"Sir. Could you please…"

I have no idea what she's asking me to do. I've always been a sucker for red lipstick openmouthed stunning magnificence. And it's not the first time that a beauty has proceeded to show me the door – the emergency exit, no less.

"Your exits are here, here and here."

Here

there

and

every

where

ooh

ah

wafting into the universe blue.

leaving England, my England.

It's only when I've been high in the sky and looked down upon my country green and pleasant that it has truly fallen upon me that I live on an island – an island of hedges and lowstone walls of clustertowns and curvyroads that lead like furred arteries to the throbbing hearts of London and Birmingham and Bristol and Liverpool and Newcastle.

When you're on the inside, it can all seem so small, this world, all bottled-up and dream restricted. But above. Well, it is pure wonderjoy.

I just happen to be on a plane this time, but I've flown many times before just sitting in a dusty chair in my little house in Tollesbury, eyes closed and flooded with lusciousness.

England fades into a whirlpool dot and the clouds now form the mass of land upon which we hoverfloat my fellow passengers and I. There's a collective trust that permeates the human air, a trust in one another and in all of humankind.

Boom and it's all over.

Boom and it all begins again.

Dukkha. Samudaya. Nirodha. Magga.

As I consider these truths, I have no idea that two Buddhas await my arrival in Borneo and that Gina and her Jazzband heroes will take me to an enlightenment glory from which I will pledge never to return.

Prajna. Sila. Samadhi.

Oh yeah.

Strange fruit indeed on the sunny side of the street.

In the back of the seat in front of me is a small, square television screen. Amazing what they can do these days. Forever having been fascinated with minutiae and replication, you can imagine my wowness when I turn it on and see a depiction of our plane and beneath it a map of the world! There are numbers that state the altitude and how many miles there are to go and, immediately, I am transfixed. There is a selection of films from which I can choose but for now it is our plane and the countries over which we fly that fires me.

Bong.

The seatbelt light blinks off. I ease my seat back and settle down to watch our little white plane traverse the skies. Within what seems like minutes, we are over France and heading across mainland Europe.

"Excuse me, sir. Would you like a drink?"

My eyes become littleboy Christmaswide for a moment until I realise that I'm being offered a choice between pineapple juice, orange juice, apple juice and water. I opt for the pineapple juice and thank the pretty lady. And then I drink it down all gulping like I'm on my knackered knees at a beer oasis. It is the most wonderful of drinks. I feel it enter my mouth and slip COLDslow down my throat, streaming off to just where it's needed within my body. As I've done so many times before, I vow to drink nothing but fresh, chilled pineapple juice for the rest of my life. I know it won't last. But what's the point of making vows if you can't keep making them?

"I'll have a pine. I'll have a pine. I'll have a pint of Stella please, barman."

Bugger.

Gentle chatter in all manner of languages is the tinkle music in the air. Then there's sleeping people, filmwatching people and others still who I'm sure are just as lost and as found as I am, gazing in silence at their little white plane as it ZX Spectrum chug chugs along. A collection of lives is all we are as we travel at two hundred miles an hour above the cornrow clouds, from the west of this earth to the east of this earth – Borneo bound and yearning.

I wonder how it is that I had always been so convinced that Italy was this side of Spain. And I just can't believe how far away Turkey is – but it is all relative, my journey having barely begun.

The further we go, the longer we fly, the less we seem to move, the more it seems the sky is thick, unyielding and remorseless, unable to prove anything but the fact that we are all lonesome. I think of my little Tollesbury and consider the nature of all things.

"Sir. Are you considering the nature of all things?"

"Yes."

"Well could you please fasten your seatbelt if that is the case."

"Of course."

"Thank you."

Red lipstick openmouthed stunning magnificence.

…in the air, in the air, in the air, in the air.

We're not birds yet we're flying. Or appearing to anyway. The little white plane on my screen seems more real to me than the fact that we are actually in the air crossing the universe blue. I can understand how the plane gets to be on the screen – but how it gets to be in the air? Well that is way beyond even my mad imagination. Who first flew and who first fell? Was it Icarus or perhaps maybe some other angel winged son? Ah Stephen Daedalus, I quite liked you in James Joyce's jottings. No wonder misery bore down upon you. No waxing lyrical when the wax just melts and the sea just gulps.

Bloomsday looms in June. But this is still April. Shower me with love and let me be on my way. Affection is affect, son. The sun is high but so am I. And I don't have wings. Not yet, anyway. So fly on, good plane, fly on. There are angel wings on the back of my calves but they won't get me any further than my seat. They're just tattoos you see. Eryn Rose, you make me smile. I'm miles high now, smiles high now.

Time moves on and we all move on. I notice on the little plane map names that glow brighter and with more force than any red lipstick.

Fallujah.

Basra.

Baghdad.

Other people are watching the latest blockbusters or listening to the poppy pop tunes of poppy popland. I'm staring at the map and closing my eyes to intensify the guiltwonder that can only come of being British or American. They should teach guiltwonder classes in school. Then may we all weep together.

I recall the scenes on the screens, the phwoosh and the glare and the red and the blue in the black and white of the flashbang sky. Torrents of rockets and bombs lighting up the horizon all deathly firework chaos. A reporter yabbering on excited, enthralled, shocked and awed, rocked and overawed. And I remember hearing silent screams and silent dread and silent children and silent mums and silent dads. I remember hearing silent whompings and silent walls breaking in silent slow-motion shudders. All is silence in my mind as if there were some muffle layer into which the bombs and rockets cracked, as if they have hit oceans and seas, not towns and cities and families and hope and historylove.

Here am I now flying over Iraq. An Englishman abroad. An Englishman appalled. I shrink in my seat in revulsion. Does a mere dotspeck aeroplane still make you quake? I'm sorry. I'm so sorry.

Forty-five minutes should ever be associated with the duration of half a game of football – not the deathlies of a lost man. That is my claim. That is my claim.

I rid my mind of the shame by spending the next two hours watching Django Unchained.

And now it's dinner time. Everything back to normal. Phew!

Oh you miniature delights of Lilliputian beauty, you wonders of the modern age. I pull down the grey tray from below my TV screen and wait regally for the hostess to place my banquet before me. I survey the scene and sit back upon my throne. There's a small white plastic cup into which I gently pour some water from an even smaller plastic cup. I start then upon a tiny roll, spreading upon it what butter I can find amidst all this miniature glory. And I chomp upon it like a Roman of oldentimes chomping upon the leg of a cow. Starters dispatched, I peel open the foil from the largest receptacle and gaze upon chicken and carrots and peas in a brown sauce. I swiftly put my plastic cutlery to use but slow down as I reach the end. I try to savour it, try so hard to eat with Buddhist mindfulness. But I'm so hungry and still so western in my ways. The dessert is some kind of cake. I don't really like it but I eat it anyway. So western in my ways.

"Would you like tea or coffee, sir?"

"Yes please."

"Tea or coffee, sir?"

"Sorry, coffee. Cheers. Black. Thanks. Cheers."

I can be so polite at times.

And just like that, the mighty meal is over. There is something about watching people eat that absorbs me. I remember once when I worked at Warley Hospital in Brentwood, a psychiatric unit of the old fashioned sort, that we had to be around when the patients got together for mealtimes – like ward reviews it could often be a flashpoint. And I would be entirely transfixed by one particular patient, a young lad, who had to be restrained most days. You'd come into work in the mornings and instead of going to the office to find out how the previous shift had been, you'd just go into his room because more often than not there would be three members of staff restraining him on the floor and you'd just take over, say goodbye to your colleague and get on with the day. But when he would eat, this lad, that was just pure majestic joy. His eyes would open so wide as he brought the forkful of food to his mouth and then he would close those very same eyes as he chewed and swallowed. And I swear he would smile whilst he chewed. But when mealtimes were over, it was back to the anger and the rage and the being restrained. He must have been about twenty-two when I knew him. The last I saw of him was when I helped take him to a secure unit in Hackney. I hope the food was alright there, I really do.

So here I am in a plane about to land at Dubai airport – still only halfway to Borneo – thinking back on my Warley days when the most incredible week of my life is still ahead of me.

Pale blue lights illuminate squares and rectangles beneath us. I blink before I realise I'm not looking down upon a technical drawing, a blueprint of a building. I have no idea what is between the rows of lights – even as we approach I am unable to prepare myself for a crash for I don't know whether we're about to come down on water or concrete or sand. It's a strange, strange moonlike feeling I feel as the wheels of the plane bumble scuff the runway and we ease slowly to a stop, having trundled up to the airport as if we had never been in the air at all.

One of the air hostesses comes over to me as it seems I'm the only one staying on the plane.

"Hello," I say.

"You need to get off now, sir."

"Oh. OK. But I'm going to Borneo. This is Dubai, isn't it?"

"This is a fuel stop-over. If you just follow everyone else and head to gate seven, we will be reboarding in an hour."

"Same seat?"

"Same seat."

"Thank you."

So I do as I am told and realise that planes aren't just buses with wings, stopping at various stops along the way for people to get on and off at will. Forty-three years old and still amazed at things like this. And may that always be the case.

I am the last to leave the plane and I walk with a stagger as I stretch my legs and ease the creaks in my knees. I don't think I have ever sat down for so long all in one go. The terminal at Dubai airport in which I find myself is huge and never ending, shiny and high and gleaming. Yet there are men and women asleep all over the floor – curled up all dressed in white, shoeless and still. I step around and over them as I make my way to gate seven. The times I have just wanted to lay myself down all come back to me now – at times of desperation and sadness, times of exhilaration and buoyancy, when the only natural action was to lie down upon the ground and close my eyes hoping that things would be altered upon awakening or that they would be cast in stone forever. I watch the white-clad figures who sleep so still before me and wonder whether they sleep in fear or in peace. I am in awe of their poise and feel a part of my being yearn to shake off my shoes and miss my flight.

But a queue is forming at gate seven and, obligingly, I join it. I am standing in a weaving line of strangers at Dubai airport, waiting patiently to enter the plane I have just left in order that I can be taken to the next stage of my journey – Brunei.

Being the optimistic fool that I am, I assume that Dubai and Brunei must be closer geographically than Dubai and London. Call it a lack of education, not paying attention or maybe just plain ignorance. Anyhow, I eventually get back to my seat to be informed by a gleeful pilot that we should be touching down in Brunei in about seven and a half hours' time. That's a whole day's cricket and more than a few football matches. I consider putting on another film but decide instead just to close my eyes and give myself up to flightville.

I awake briefly and we are over India. I drowsy sleep back into crickety dreams and the next time I awake we are descending into Brunei. I check the screen in front of me and see that it is just gone four in the afternoon. I think it's Tuesday but I'm not sure. And it is at that point when I give up wondering what time it is back in England.

"Welcome to Brunei. Would all passengers please be aware that the importation of drugs into Brunei is punishable by death."

Welcome indeed.

As I get off the plane, a man walking in front of me takes off his denim jacket, drapes it over a railing and continues walking towards the arrivals area. I think of all the reasons he may have discarded this article of clothing and feel the fragility of life, the finality of death.

I was once asked to review the psychiatric notes of a man who was at the time on death row in Thailand for drug offences. It remains to this day one of the most difficult tasks I have ever undertaken. I have never met the man and I don't know to this day whether they killed him or not.

I'm shaking a little as I enter Brunei airport.

Brunei is on the North West Coast of Borneo – the Sabah region to the North East is my final destination. My day is nearing an end. Just one more flight – from Brunei to Kota Kinabalu – a thirty minute flight that passes without event. And at last my feet touch Malaysian soil.

2. Leave the Smeary Smoke to those that would Inhale

I can sense the heat though I am not yet in the heat. I can sense change though I am yet to be changed. I am tired for sure, but in a wide-eyed sleepychild way. I queue up at the window where you buy your taxi tickets and wait by the side of the road to be ushered into a taxi. I don't have to wait long before a smiling man leaps towards me, grabs my heavy case with incredible ease, hurls it into the boot of his taxi and opens the passenger door, waving me in with a gusto unsurpassed. Before I have even managed to put on my seatbelt, I am being driven into the Kota Kinabalu evening.

"Australian?" the driver asks me through his grin.

"No. English."

"Ah Wayne Rooney!"

I nod and smile, marvelling at the breadth of the beautiful game. I consider telling him about my love of Dagenham & Redbridge but decide against it.

I look out of the window of the taxi as it eases through the streets. There is not a lot of traffic and hardly anybody to be seen. I look at the clock on the dashboard and see that it is just gone half past seven. I have no idea where my hotel is in relation to the airport – just that it cost me thirty Ringgits – about six pounds. Wouldn't get you to the end of your road in London.

Half an hour after getting into the taxi we finally pull up outside Hotel Eden 54 – the hotel where I will spend one night before disappearing into the oldest rain forest in the world. And I can't help but notice, as my driver leaps out, bangs open the boot and swings my suitcase towards me, that adjacent to the hotel is a shop – still open – called Tong Hing's Wine Shop. Bless you Tong Hing!

What am I doing? I am in Borneo – on the other side of the world, yet still the sight of an off-licence causes my heart to thump. But I make no apologies for that. It's forgiveness on all sides. Get in!

I once ran loudly upstairs and awoke my wife in the midst of her golden slumbers just so I could tell her that there was a three for two bottle of wine offer at the corner shop at the end of the road. The news had little impact upon her other than to cause her to slowly shake her head and mumble bewail my very existence. Some people just do not know a bargain when they see one.

But I'm in Borneo now. And already I'm beginning to love it.

The entrance to Eden 54 gives way to a small white room occupied by a beaming man whose willingness to relieve me of my cases gives rise to immediate anxiety on my part, followed by sweet relief as I follow him up a flight of steep stairs to the reception area. He wishes me a fine stay and then swiftly returns to his post at the foot of the stairs. I wonder how long he was waiting before I arrived and whether or not I should have tipped him. The confusion on my face merely seems to induce pity in the woman at the reception desk.

"Are you OK, sir?"

"Yeah I think so."

"Do you have a reservation?"

"Yep. Just for tonight."

"Can I have your name, please?"

"Stuart Ayris."

She types my name into her computer and hands me a key – no checking of passport or debit cards or anything like that. I look about me and see that opposite the reception desk is a lounge of sorts – several comfy looking chairs set around small square tables. And to the right is a bright and welcoming bar. I hear English voices from the far end of the bar but there is no music, no music at all.

"Have I already paid for the room? Just I can't remember. Complicated all this travelling business."

The receptionist taps her computer keyboard a couple of times, turns back to me and nod smiles.

"Good stuff."

"You'll be in room 101 – which is just there."

The receptionist points to her left and there indeed is a door with the number 101 upon it. Room 101. Strange but true. Shudder not Winston mate for I enter it with a full heart and brimming with love. 1984 is long gone. Margaret Thatcher is long gone. And so are Wham!. Shudder not.

"Would you like a wake-up call in the morning before you go-go sir?"

"That'd be good. Cheers. Need to leave at ten I think to get a taxi to the airport. Could you book one for us?"

"Of course."

"Cheers. Lovely, then. I'll get going to my room."

Why I told her this, I have no idea, but get going I did anyway, dragging my wheely case behind me as if it were a smitten conquest from the caveman wild.

My room comprises a single bed, a chest of drawers with a small television upon it and a bathroom. But all these things barely register, for I am drawn to a big and magical window through which Kota Kinabalu simmers.

There's films and heat and James Bond and far away worldlands. There's different coloured skies and there's wind that isn't even wind. As I look through my big window it's like I'm seeing a close up star that has detail and sway and colour and definition. Why shine far away when you can shimmer shimmer right before me? Dance on if dance it be. Or maybe it's me just looking through a window. It's all the same.

I see straight layers. There's the grey white of the road and the shadow of the pavement then the bright bawdiness of an advertising hoarding declaring that Coca Cola is the ultimate answer. Above that is the encroaching green of greenery, smirking and sniggering knowing that in truth the ultimate answer is not Coca Cola or any other soft drink for that matter. Then there is a variable blue just beneath a white cloudy fuzz and through and above all, above everything towers the rocky, granite stone monolith that is Mount Kinabalu.

All through my window. Pointing up to heaven.

Mount Kinabalu.

Craters and crash and crusts have thrust these mountains through the surface of this earth to dominate our vistas all over, all over. Climb on and up you valour chaps and you gap year youngsters but leave me to the view if you please. Dot not the perfect lines with your bravura. If there is a fly on the rim of my glass let it not be you. Slip, slide away to the very stem and leave the smeary smoke to those that would inhale.

Are you on the plane still?
Nope.
Where are you then?
Hotel. Just a hotel.
Slip inside the wine of your mind
then you might…

Tong Hing's Wine Shop is just a double step leap down the stairs and a turn to the right. Once inside I am bright light magnetised. The hum from the fridges soothes me like row upon row of Buddha smile noddings. I get myself some wine, screwtop too, and all is fine. Just one bottle, for just one night. Oh traveller me.

And then I do my best to snuggle in my single bed all quiltless (just sheets!) and am brought down to grim humbly earth with the realisation that there is indeed, surely must be, a pea beneath my slender mattress. Oh traveller me? More like a princess at this stage, so early in my journey, so surly in my sojourn.

The night lies yearning.

Try as I might, I cannot find that pesky pea. So sleepless I awake to the Borneo dawn, ill-tempered and still to shake the vestiges of western privilege from these ostensibly austere Dagenham bones. Western is as western does. Oh my. But morning it is. And my eyes are ever so slowly widening.

The telephone beside my bed rings three times and then stops. I briefly wonder at the perseverance of the many debt collection companies that dog my existence – Wescott, Apex, First Direct to name but the latest few – when I realise the ringing of the phone must be my wake-up call. My heartbeat slows and I sigh, jump in the shower quickly to rid myself of the surly spectre of debt collectors and put on the same t-shirt and shorts that I wore yesterday. I'd seen no sense in unpacking, reasoning that this stay at Eden 54 was only ever intended to be an indulgent stop-over nap.

So I pick up my case and bid farewell to my room.

"Goodbye bed and room and window."

No sooner have I stepped out into the lobby than the lady at reception calls over to let me know that my taxi driver is downstairs waiting to take me back to Kota Kinabalu airport. From there I'll get an internal flight east to Sandakan airport and on to Sepilok.

I struggle down the stairs to meet my driver and am a little disappointed that it is a different one from yesterday. I hope it doesn't show for it seems *he* is a little disappointed that he has not been given the opportunity to help me down with my suitcase.

"Hello!" he bellows. "I take your case. You rest. Follow me. To the airport?"

I nod and do as I am told.

With a click and a heave my case is in the boot and within moments I am being whisked back through the streets that only fifteen hours before had seen me travelling in the opposite direction.

"You American?" the driver asks me, grinning into his mirror.

"No. English."

"England long way!"

"Yeah."

I close my eyes for a while and then feel annoyed that I may have missed some vital sight or other, some spark that would ignite me, thrill me into enlightenment. But then I forgive myself and berate my foolish mind for its harshness. And then I forgive myself again for my mind beratings. You can't beat a bit of practice – especially where forgiving is concerned.

I wearywalk into the airport and sit down to await the flight to Sandakan. The departure area consists of several rows of white plastic chairs and a large window beyond which is the airfield. There are only a few people there when I arrive but the chairs soon fill up and before long it's standing room only. As I look about I really do feel that I am at the edge of the world. I am so clearly the only westerner. There is a peace amongst my fellow travellers, a peace to which I am unaccustomed when surrounded by strangers back in England. I sense not my usual feeling of panic and terror. It is as if I am the only one here that is aware of my presence. Or is it just radical acceptance? Who knows?

There have been times when I have been scared alone and terrified within a crowd, moments where I have sensed only dread when close to people I don't know. I have a constant vision of living alone outside of society, happily tending a plot of land somewhere out of reach of modern day stresses. Just last week though I almost went insane when Sky Sports decided to go down whilst I was watching the cricket. I guess I still have a way to go yet.

It is whilst I am pondering the vicissitudes of my strange life that an announcement is made in perfect English informing us all that the plane is ready for boarding. There is none of the frantic positioning and unseemly jostle usually associated with such activities – but merely a gentle reconfiguring of bodies that just enhances the coolness of the scene and my burgeoning fascination for Borneo and its people.

Once on the plane, I clunk click myself into the seat and gaze at the air hostess as she performs so shyly the safety instructions. I want to tell her that everything will be alright, that we'll all be OK. But instead I just hum a tune of my own devising to distract myself from her beauty. When she finishes I see her lips part a little as she sighs a soft sigh maybe of relief or perhaps boredom at being ogled at by one such as I. Immediately I am ashamed and resume my humming, somewhat louder this time, just to prove to all onlookers that I have already moved on from our brief relationship.

To my surprise, as the engines rumble into being, a cold mist is pumped throughout the plane through vents just beneath the overhead lockers. It is only then that I realise just how intense is the heat and humidity all about me. I am cooled and calmed and soothed within moments, closing my eyes to the white mist as if I am a mountain and the mist is bursts of upper heaven clouds. So enthralled am I, I don't even notice we have taken off until I open my eyes and see the northern coastline of Borneo falling away into the South China Seas.

Half an hour later I am being welcomed to Sandakan airport by huge, wonderful pictures depicting Sepilok Jungle Resort. And once through customs the true light does shine down upon me.

It's like I'm in an aircraft hangar church. The roof so high and angular above me forms triangle after triangle of steel struts and short ribs. My too wide eyes are drawn to the end and it is only then that I am bathed in suncolour beams of red and pale green and blue and gold. It is magnificent and baptismal. I feel cleansed of all that has gone before and await with a clean slate all that is to come. My soul stays. All else is shaken off like so much dust. My heart beats not with blood but with love. And my body disintegrates about me. A smiling woman with the roundest face and yellowest outfit I ever saw slideshuffles over to me with a broom in one hand, a piece of board in the other. She winks at me, brushes my fragmented bones and discarded, redundant skin into an apologetic pile and nudges it onto the board.

"Will that be all, sir?" she enquires, all sultry gorgeous.

She waits not for an answer.

For she knows I have no answer to give.

Red and pale green and blue and gold is all I know just now.

Somehow, the next thing I recall is that I am standing at a reception desk in the lobby of Sepilok Jungle Resort. I have no idea whether I am indoors or outside. It looks nothing like the posters I saw at the airport.

And for the first time in my life, I breathe, really breathe.

"Do you have a reservation, sir?"

I smile.

And breathe again.

"None at all," I say whisper. "None at all."

Buddha me up people.

                      Buddha me up.

3. This Gorgeous Wild Madness

Having checked in, I open the door to the left of the reception area and expect (foolish me!) to find some sort of corridor that will lead me to my room. But instead, I do believe I have entered dreamland.

I'm on a wooden slatted platform that leads off to my right and to my left. And before me, well, what I see stuns me into action. I know that if I stand there any longer than a second, I will possibly never move again. I am saved by a small sign that indicates my room is to the right. I scuttle off in that direction, my case rumbling dully along the slats until I reach a door that opens into a stone building.

The lack of light makes me realise just how bright it is outside. I slow my pace and hope my thudding heart takes heed. I walk on until I find my room number – fifty-six. I turn my key in the lock and hurl my suitcase into the room before closing the door. I check that it's locked but it just keeps opening. I try every combination of key and handleturn but still the door relents whenever I give it a slight nudge. Finally, I realise I have to flick the little button on the inside and yep the door locks behind me.

Like a boy finally released into the beautywonder of the six weeks holidays I am unencumbered and gone, gone chasing down the stone corridor to the heat and the glory of the Borneo outerdoors.

I look first up at the mid-afternoon sky and it is pure white – none of that ZX Spectrum Cyan, just pure and perfect white. So where is this heat coming from, this hot,

hot heat that feels just right? Lowering my eyes, I see the tip top central slim green archstone of a semi-circle curve. It's the top of a tree that I see, a perfect head-dress curve, Red Indian but not red but green. They may be leaves and they may be fruit, perhaps static birds asleep and resting. I just don't know. I've never seen anything like it before in my life. And from the edges there are slender line spokes that feed in towards a central pokerfaced, eyeless, mouthless fulcrum. But there's no pivot or lever or waft and sway here. Just perfect stillness, an emerald peacock eye unblinking amidst static shooting stars held in motion by the white, the pure white of the sky. And all this is held aloft by the straightest, smoothest treetrunk you ever saw. Tall and majestic, village lamppost beautiful. The trunk extends from a grassy disc some fifteen feet across, a disc that seems to float upon the shiny mud waters of this Sepilok retreat.

And in my mind I hear one of my boys whisper to me: "It's just a tree, Dad."

I wish they were here. But they're not. One of those things.

I could leave right now and be fulfilled. But I've only just arrived. And I'm yet to meet Robert.

"Robert! Robert! Robert!"

I am drawn from my reverie by the high pitched sound of a woman calling.

"Robert! Robert! Robert!"

The sound is coming from my left and so I walk down the wooden planks in the direction of the call. I'm not Robert. I know that. But I wonder if he's in trouble and could do with some help. Just what I'll do when I get there, I don't know. Already everything is feeling unreal and dreamlike. Could be the heat or it could be the fact I haven't eaten for a while. Maybe, I think to myself, it's because I haven't *drunk* for a while. I'm OK though because this wooden walkway bridge isn't swaying and nothing is moving but me. Within minutes I am faced with a sign welcoming me to The Banana Restaurant. Everything is quiet and I am still outside. Yet somehow I am now in The Banana Restaurant, a large canopy covered area complete with small tables, a bar (closed!) and several people seated in the far corner, seemingly oblivious to my arrival. Where Robert is, or indeed the woman who called for him, I do not know.

I'm outside and inside all at the same time. Were it not for the high wooden roof and the wooden floor, I feel I would be about to sup in the jungle itself. All around me is the scratch kneerub scratch sound of crickets, the caw of birds I have yet to see and as many shades of green as any eye could ever behold.

A small, smiling man pads over on bare feet to my bewildered self and asks me where I'd like to sit. I tell him that I don't really mind and he leads me to a table adjacent to a wooden rail that has clearly been erected to stop fools such as I leaning over and thwap splashing into the shimmering brown green waters below.

I sit down and slip off my trainers. I never wear socks except for unspecial occasions and feel electrified as the soles of my feet gently caress the wooden slats beneath them. It's like I have suddenly become a part of the whole bare structure, this strangeness, this gorgeous wild madness on the other side of the world.

In the far corner I see that the group of people I had earlier noticed consists of two men, a child of about five years old and three women. They're all playing some sort of game, perhaps cards or something and each has every kind of smile upon his or her face. There's the beaming smile, the cheeky smile, at least two wondersmiles (the best in my opinion!) and everything in between. The tension they radiate is good tension and just as I'm about to turn away to look at the laminated menu on my table, that tension erupts into absolute laughter. I have no idea who has won – if indeed anybody has won – just that as a result the air above and around me is suffused with the joy of good people. I feel entirely safe. Until I look at the menu.

I recognise a burger and chips but dismiss it immediately. I haven't come all this way for burger and chips. But as for the rest of the fare on offer, I have no idea what it consists of. I don't recognise anything other than noodly type things. Ah if only I had my Reinhardt dice with me, then all this anguish would dissipate. Not that it's really anguish of course. It's just me sitting here working out what to eat. A lady comes over, gleamsmiles at me and asks me if I am ready to order.

"What sort of drinks do you have?"

"We have Tiger beer and other things."

"Tiger beer then, please."

"And to eat?"

"I don't really know. What do you think?"

"It's all good."

"OK then," I say. "I'll have this, please." I point to a picture of some yellowish looking noodles and what looks like chopped tomatoes. A safe bet I reckon.

"Thank you," she says, sauntering away soundlessly across the wooden platform and through a doorway next to the merrymakers in joy corner.

Ah how I want whisky before me on this sultry afternoon. How I want it to burn the back of my throat, for its flames to flicker orange through my mind. But it's not to be. My musings are disturbed by a small boy who skips bare foot over to me and presents me with a small can of Tiger beer. It's sweating cold drips at least. I look for the alcohol percentage amidst the small print on the blue can. I'm guessing this tiger roars around 4%. Where are you my cheap whisky beast? But is that the old me? Have I come all this way to be transformed or to have my principles validated? I certainly haven't come here to get wasted on whisky and wine. And I remind myself of that as I sip upon my tiny can.

And still no sign of Robert – whoever he is, wherever he may be.

I close my eyes before the humid heat and do my best to slip into the stream of the scene. I feel first my breath within my lungs as I breathe in. It's better than this beer, I can tell you. And as I breathe out I am aware that the air within me has now merged with the air around me, the world around me, this foreign, unreal world of green and woodthwack and blue sky and swamp and smiles. I feel my eyelids quiver and I sense the gap between my splayed fingers as they rest upon my keg of a belly. I have a t-shirt on though for it's not my mission to scare the children. Not like when I was a road sweeper in Romford many years ago when I would take juvenile delight in emitting a low rumbleroar just within earshot of those poor boys and girls who were being dragged by a parent hand through town. It was a skill I honed to an amazing degree, that modulation of tone that no adult could detect. But my scaring children days are long gone. Still makes me smile to think of it though. And I still struggle at times to get adults to hear me.

It isn't just by the opening of my eyes that I find my senses heightened. Everything seems sharper. Perhaps the breathing in was more significant than the breathing out. What is undeniable though is that a bowl has been placed before me and the noodly contents smell delicious. Steam rises as if to meet my salivations and I tuck right on in. It tastes alright, not great. There's not a lot of flavour and it's all a bit soggy for my liking. But I hope it doesn't show on my face. The noodles fill me up though and that's when I understand that perhaps in these parts that is the role of food – to sustain, not to entertain, to nourish, not to augment. I promise myself that next time I eat it will be with a deal more wonderment and mindfulness than the scoffing that just sullied this timidly honest place.

"Robert! Robert! Come here, Robert!"

I look up from my bowl and see the woman that had served my drink leaning over the wooden fence. Thinking someone could actually be in the swampy waters below I stand and move to her side, unsure as to what I would do were Robert to be drowning and not waving.

But I needn't be concerned. For he is neither drowning nor waving. He is flying, flying up towards the branch of a tree that hangs within a foot of where we stand.

So far from gazing upon the flailing limbs and desperate visage of a struggling man, I am looking upon a now stationary Stork-Billed Kingfisher. Robert is almost six inches in height and is absolutely still upon his branchy perch. He grips it with bright red talons that extend from his yellow body. His wings are all kinds of blue from bright electric through to deep dark navy just depending on how the sunbeams catch them. And protruding from his stocky head is an orange red beak that must be in length half the size of his body. Between the brown eyes either side of the beak is a smudge of black that fades to grey and merges into yellow as it recedes. I wait for him to do something but he just sits there.

"Hello, Robert!" calls the lady beside me. "You want breakfast?"

Still Robert just clings to the branch, as if it is his grip alone that is keeping the entire tree upright. Is he embarrassed by my ladyfriend's attentions? Or does he just know what's coming?

As I am thinking upon the potential emotions that Robert is experiencing, errant pieces of bread are flung from beside me to flop and float on the muddy waters. Soggy bread. Not quite the fish, frogs, crabs and rodents this fragile colourful delight is used to. But he does, to give him credit, make an effort to stumble from the branch and flap laboriously down to snatch up a chunk of bread.

"Good boy, Robert! Good boy!"

Robert emits a short shrill in response.

It could be *thank you*. Or it could be *fuck you*. I like to think that perhaps he is proffering forgiveness to his excitable benefactor. Of course it could be that he is just a bird making a bird sound.

I resume my seat, drink a few more cans of Tiger beer and find myself becoming increasingly drowsy. The sultry early evening heat melts into me, becomes a part of me and I am constantly lifting the sweat soaked fabric of my t-shirt from my sodden body. I wander over towards where the gaggle of happy people are still playing their game in the far corner and ask for the bill. One of them understands and I settle up, having little idea what I have actually paid for and whether the colourful notes I handed over were too little or too much. The people continue with their game almost immediately so I figure the transaction is done.

When I'm almost at the door that leads to the rooms, a cheer wafts through the air. Are these people never sad? I think to myself. Still, I can imagine poor Robert, perhaps in the shade now, on the lookout for a lost frog or something, wondering how it is that humans can be so, well, undignified – the bread-throwing lady humouring me whilst Robert humours them. It's a strange old, mixed up world at times. Perhaps the secret is to be aware of that and just to let it all flow, flow, flow.

Keep patting the donkey.

Once in my room, I head for the bed and am dead to the world till morning. This travelling business is more tiring than ever I imagined. It could be the heat and it could be the humidity. Or maybe it's the unconscious effort necessary to take in all that is around me.

I awake still tired but satisfied. I've just spent my first night close to the Borneo jungle – and survived! What an adventurer I am! I try out the shower and it is wonderfully cold. I imagine I am Paul Newman or Robert Redford in an old cowboy film, covered in dust then the dust washed clean. But there's cold and there's cold. I dry myself rapidly with a small towel and note that already there is redness upon my body where there hadn't been before. There is a distinct discolouration halfway up my upper arms and just above my knees. Some may call it red.

I have no real idea what time it is but I'm aware from looking out of my window that the sun has not been long in rising. I have always somehow been able to be accurate almost to the minute when it comes to judging the time of day. This particular ability has probably evolved over the years as a means of combatting my long-standing fear of being late for even the most trivial of occasions. Out here in jungleland (down in Jungle Land!!!) I judge it to be quite a handy ability to have. I know I am due to meet the guide that will accompany me and several others for the next six days at some time around seven o'clock so packing my bags I say goodbye to the second room of my trip, a room that really just saw me asleep and snorey and head over to the reception area, dragging my suitcase behind me.

"Hello, sir."

"Hi."

"Are you checking out?"

"Yeah. Supposed to be meeting a guide or something. What time is it?"

"Just before seven. Your guide is there."

The beautiful receptionist nods her head in the direction of a man who is lying on one of the floral sofas. He has dark hair, a dark complexion, wears a white t-shirt and tan shorts down to his knees. His feet are bare and the lamp that hangs from the ceiling lights up his big round sunglasses. I'm not sure whether to wake him or not. I don't even know if he's awake or not behind his shades. As I clear my throat in order to speak, he sits up in one smooth motion and lowers his sunglasses to the bridge of his nose.

"I'm Tom Cruise," he says, smiling. "Our driver is outside by the bus. His name is Cheng."

At that moment, a wrinkled round bespectacled face peers out from behind the doorframe that opens out into the sand dust parking area. The grin on that face, all gap-toothed and joyous is something I'll never forget.

"He no Tom Cruise," barks Cheng. "He say that to all the ladies! His name is Faz. No Tom Cruise."

"That's Cheng there," says my guide, smiling now as he stands. "He thinks he's Steve McQueen. Let's go. He doesn't like to be kept waiting."

Faz and Cheng.

The Buddhas of Borneo.

Oh yeah.

Here we go.

4. Western Shackles

The bus is a seven seater (not counting Faz and Cheng who are in the passenger and driver's seat respectively) yet I am clearly the only other occupant.

"Are we picking the others up on the way?"

Faz turns to look at me, smiles and lowers his sunglasses slightly.

"You are the others," he says.

"I am the others?"

"Probably."

I decide that further conversation will only confuse me so I return his smile with one of my own. The word *probably* will always remind me of Faz.

Given the Foreign Office warnings about travelling here, particular to this part of Borneo, I may be forgiven for thinking that I have just been kidnapped. Are they taking me to some distant shore where I will be transported by open topped boat to an island that isn't even on any map for some sort of ransom demand? I think of how much an English mental health nurse may fetch and struggle to come up with a figure. It is whilst I am debating in my mind as to whether or not I would fetch as much as a dentist, that Faz turns to speak to me again.

"So," he says. "First we'll be going to the Sandakan Memorial Park then onto the local indoor market. Then we will go to the Buddhist temple and after that onto the batcave."

"The batcave?" I ask, clearly the whole kidnap idea not having fully left my mind.

"Yes. To see the bats."

"Ah OK."

"All good?"

"All good."

"So I'm kind of on this tour on my own? For the next five days?"

Faz nods.

"Good stuff," I say. "Will you and Cheng be with me all the way?"

"All the way."

I have barely known them for ten minutes yet I feel entirely reassured. I'll be alright with these two. I have no idea why. Perhaps I don't yet possess the capacity to understand.

"It will be alright, won't it?" I ask. "What with the recent troubles and stuff."

Faz doesn't turn to face me this time when he speaks, but instead looks across to Cheng.

"Probably," they both say in unison.

I'm about to ask another question when Cheng turns up the radio and floors the accelerator. I see him grinning in the rear view mirror. Faz is mouthing the words to Madonna's "Like a Virgin" and the bus is doing its best to remain in one piece as it bumps and blams down this dirt track of a road.

Faz and Cheng seem comfortable in silence. I get the sense that they have spent many hours together. There's probably thirty years between them I reckon – Faz is possibly mid-twenties and Cheng close to sixty – yet it is as if their age is all that distinguishes the one from the other. I have five days with them and already feel that this could all be something special. I'm not going to get kidnapped – not by these two at least. It will take me a while to shake off my western shackles, my imperial cynicism and stand-offish ways, but I make it my mission, within the next week, to be as cool as the two men that are sitting there in front of me. I feel I have been given an opportunity here, a chance to learn how really to be. The fact that I am the only member of the tour party, well that can only be a sign. I have no time to waste. Why stare out of the window when I could be engaging with Faz and Cheng?

"Sorry, Faz," I say, leaning forward. "Just wanted to say how amazed I am at how kind of English things are from what I've seen. You know, how so many people speak it, the adverts on the hoardings and that. You even drive on the same side of the road as we do."

"Only on the dirt tracks."

"What?"

"The dirt tracks. We only drive on the left side on the dirt tracks. When we get on the big roads, the tarmac ones, we drive on the right side."

"Blimey. That's mad."

"Yes. Yes it is."

I sit back and wonder at the skill of the drivers, of people like Cheng who are not only able to cross the country on mud roads that, as far as I can see, have no signposts whatsoever, but are also able to alter their perception with the flick of a switch, to drive at times on the right and other times on the left.

"No listen to him," says Cheng, turning to face me as the bus hurtles forward still. "He tell same joke every time."

I hear Faz giggle. Cheng grins across at him. And I see already that I have so much to learn.

Now I'm forty-three years old and have always had a fascination for history, a deep yearning to appreciate more how lives were lived many years ago. I don't believe in countries or nations, in men or women. I guess I have just come to believe in moments, timeless moments during which it is not the earth that turns but I. Easy when you've had a drink, continue to drink and fool yourself into thinking that the only way of entering such a state is to drink increasingly more. It's a hard old thing to accept that you can't carry on like that. And this is what I'm thinking as we pull up on the side of a road and Faz eases from the passenger seat to get out and slide open my door. Cheng stays where he is. Clearly he's not coming.

"Sandakan Memorial Park," says Faz as he leads me through the entrance.

Almost immediately a different sort of silence abounds, a hush so lush it's like I have to slow my pace just to get anywhere at all. Faz moves ahead of me, turning intermittently to check I'm still here, still in this century. But I don't think I am. I feel myself merging with the trees and the shrubs that line the path upon which my footsteps noiselessly fall. My flip-flops feel like they are betraying me, an unnecessary encumbrance that serve only to distance me from this experience. I remove them and resolve to utilise footwear in the future only when the situation truly demands it. And it's not here, not now. I place them to the side of the path and hope never to see them again.

Along the pathway, there are square signs with writing upon them. I'd love to stand and read them but my eyes are drawn above and beyond them to the tall trees and the slashes of sunlight, vision beyond vision. And I'm also worried that I may lose Faz. I can still see him ahead of me though so it's OK. So quickly have I come to view Faz as a symbol of safety. For as long as he's around I think I'll be alright, despite the fact that right now I can almost hear my heart beating. It is as if the dense silence all around me has somehow amplified the natural thuddings within my very body.

When I catch up with Faz, having turned a corner, I see that he is leaning against the doorframe of a wooden building. The structure is fronted by a veranda with steps made from planks of wood leading to the entrance. The doorway is about six feet wide and eight feet tall – taking up a third of the façade. The uppermost horizontal beam above the doorway forms the base of three struts that fan out from the centre in some desperate attempt perhaps to emulate the trees from which they had once been hewn. Their job now though is to help support the apex of the roof which hangs down low each side forming a perfect triangle. It is all symmetrical beauty yet it feels so much a part of the natural order of which the park comprises. It is just like a different kind of tree, an as yet unnamed tree that has sprung fully formed from the midst of this Sandakan ground.

"This is the pavilion," Faz tells me. "Go in, take your time. We have lots of time." He smiles whenever he talks. He nods to a small woman who is sitting unmoving on a stool to the right of the doorway. "I'll sign your name in. Like I said, take your time."

It is when I am inside and the sunlight fails to follow me in, I become aware of just what a place I am in. For this whole park, this entire area, was once a Prisoner of War Camp. The pavilion tells its story by way of photographs, quotes from some of those involved and statements of just what actually occurred. I walked into that pavilion one man, and I walked out an hour later quite another. Well not entirely altered – that would be too dramatic even for me. It changed me though, fortifying me in some ways, deeply saddening me in others. But did I feel lighter on leaving than on arrival? Yes. I did. Not quite light enough to fly just yet, but certainly getting there.

The dates and numbers first, for it is they that frame me exactly where I stand, as if they are hovering in the air having peeled themselves from their respective boards to pin me in position just so as I take notice. But I can't grasp them right now even to put down on paper. They are too abstract, so devoid of the emotions that brought them into being – anger, hatred, servitude, power – but most of all courage.

Between the eighth and the fifteenth of February 1942, a battle was fought in Singapore known as The Fall of Singapore. When the Japanese invaded, 80,000 British, Indian and Australian troops were captured. The destination for some of them over the ensuing years would be the Prisoner of War Camp in Sandakan, on the grounds upon which I now stand more than seventy years later.

I think of my grandad, for he fought in the Second World War. I think he was based in North Africa, so many miles from home. I've seen one or two pictures of him from those times. He is not with us any longer (not in physical form anyhow). He made my brother and me a wooden fort for our cowboys and Indians all entirely by hand. I remember how we always had to be silent when eating at the dinner table whenever we went round – which was frequent as for a long time we lived in the same street. I recall that his hearing was never very good and how he would wear headphones that were plugged into the television.

Standing here in Sandakan POW Camp I want to cry. I wish I had taken the time to know my grandad better. I love him and I miss him.

"Mummy?"

"Yes, love."

"Why can't Grandad hear very well?"

"He just can't, love."

"But his ears are really big. Why is that?"

"It's from when he was a soldier. His helmet was too big and made his ears stick out because it rested on them."

"Oh."

"Well that's what he told me when I was a little girl anyway…"

I try to compose myself as I move slowly around the room reading the information on the boards until I arrive at the section detailing what are referred to as The Death Marches. With the airstrip at Sandakan completed, the prisoners remained at the camp until the Allies bombed the airfield at Sandakan in January 1945.

470 troops from the camp were selected to carry munitions and equipment to the western coast of Borneo so the Japanese army could relocate. The march to the town of Ranau, through marshes and then jungleland followed by an ascent up the eastern slope of Mount Kinabalu took nine days during which 161 miles were covered. The prisoners received only sufficient rations for four days and many would already have spent the previous two or three years living in hostile and unsanitary conditions, with little food and even less hope.

By 26th June 1945, only six of the original group of 470 prisoners were still alive – five Australian soldiers and one British soldier. Most of their friends and colleagues had either died from malnutrition or dysentery. Others, too unfit to continue, had been shot and left by the roadside.

As I read this, I think of my first night in Borneo at Eden 64, looking out of my window at Mount Kinabalu and that cold can of beer I drank so greedily.

The second of the three death marches began on 29th May 1945 where 536 of the remaining men at the Sandakan POW Camp were marched to the new base at Ranau. This march took twenty-six days with 183 of the men making it to join the six men that had survived the first death march. A third and final march, to empty the Sandakan POW Camp took place just after the second march began. This comprised seventy-five of the remaining 250 prisoners. None of them made it more than thirty-one miles out of Sandakan, so malnourished and ill were they. Those who didn't die of natural causes were killed. The same was the case for those men left back at the camp.

In Europe, the Germans had surrendered unconditionally on 8th May 1945 – the Japanese would not follow suit until 15th August of the same year, by which time all the men at Sandakan POW Camp had perished. Only thirty-eight survived at Ranau by the end of July. And by the end of August they too had either died or been killed.

I have almost completed my tour of this long room, having started off down the left hand side, moved by an intricate model of the Sandakan POW Camp at the far end and now here I am with just a few boards left to read, a few photographs left to see. I'm not sure I can take much more. I feel like I have witnessed all the tragedy I have read about right there in front of me. The fact that I am standing on the grounds of the POW Camp, well that just brings so much forth within me – shame, disgust, horror, fear. What a man can do to a man. What a man can do to a man.

And they call this a holiday?

I lift my eyes one final time and see six photographs of six young Australians – men that escaped during the time the POW Camp was in operation. Just six young men. The only ones that ever made it out.

Gunner Owen Campbell and Bombardier Richard Braithwaite escaped into the jungle during the second death march. Private Nelson Short, Warrant Officer William Sticpewich, Private Keith Botterill and Lance Bombardier William Moxham managed to escape from Ranau during July 1945.

I look upon their faces and read some of the quotes attributed to them, what they'd witnessed, experienced, undergone.

The sunlight through the doorway creeps towards my bare feet, beckoning me back outside into the brightness and the beauty of this Borneo day. Faz leads me gently back along the path and speaks not a word. I have nothing to say anyhow. I have tears in my eyes the entire way – for my grandad, for those men that lived, those men that died, tears for all men and for that of which only man is capable.

Once back in the van, Faz hands me a bottle of cold water and turns to Cheng.

"Next stop, Sandakan Market," he says.

"How you like the park?" Cheng asks me as he guns the engine within an inch of its precarious life.

"I don't know," I reply.

"Me as well," he says, "and I been there hundred times."

"I was just thinking, Faz, how hard it must be for the Japanese visitors to read all that. Do you get many coming?"

"They're the ones I go in with," he replies.

I sit for the next hour at the back of the bus with one hand across my forehead, gazing out of the window occasionally, doing my best to cry only when Cheng is swearing loudly at drivers who he judges to be even more reckless than he is.

5. Shopping Knee and Majesty

"You OK?" Faz turns and asks me.

"Yep."

"Plan now is we drop you off at the market in Sandakan. You can look around for half an hour and then to the Buddhist temple."

I nod. It sounds like a lot to do. It's only midday and I'm exhausted already – a combination of the humidity, the prisoner of war camp and, to be honest, just being so far away from Tollesbury. When I was younger I used to carry my guitar with me wherever I went. I bought it when I was fourteen years old from the money I earned working at Charlie Fancourt's Fish Emporium in Romford Market. It barely left my sight. I'd never play it when I went away, but just its presence made me feel that things would be alright. If the worst were to happen, I still had my guitar. Seven pounds a week I earned at the time. Seven fishy pounds from the age of twelve until I was seventeen. No raise, no discussion. Even when pound coins were introduced in 1983, none ever crossed my palm from Charlie. He paid me in single pound notes all the way through to the time I got a job in an insurance company. The pound note was withdrawn from circulation in March 1988 when I was nineteen years old and the thought of it still holds a strange place within me.

I check in my pockets and pull out my Borneo money. The colours are wonderful and I gaze upon each note as if they are entirely alien to me. Ringgits they're called and beautiful they are. I know how much English money I changed up back in Tesco in Maldon and feel suddenly self-conscious for I have no idea of the cost of living over here. I could be holding more in my hand than Faz and Cheng earn in a month or a year. For someone who considers himself an internationalist, there are times when I realise I know nothing about the world at all.

My self-pity is interrupted by Cheng's hefty braking and Faz sliding open my door.

"Are you coming?" I ask as I stumble out.

Faz shakes his head and jumps back into the passenger seat. "We'll just be over the road," he tells me.

So here I am, standing in front of the indoor market. It feels like I am at an old cinema, the type I used to queue up around the block to get into when I was a young boy growing up in Romford. But there are no films on display here as I look up at the large sign that is held up between two square yellow pillars, pillars that rise up from the ground, through the curved iron canopy and up to the roof.

Pasar Umum Sandakan – Sandakan Central Market

There are some benches scattered about the front upon which there are quiet people sitting. As I glance across, it seems they are all individually on the verge of smiling, their eyes unblinking as they stare into the street. There is a calmness in the air, a softness of spirit that renders me instantly at ease. Entering the market, I do my best to open up all my senses, to breathe in and breathe out in order that I may become more than a mere observer.

I'm the squish of the squash of the lolloping yellow fruit that once dangled from a branch and now just *displays* itself upon a cracked old wooden table. I'm the heat of the spindly chillies that are crammed into sacks about my feet, such heat as would burn off the arm of a man to the elbow should he be so foolish to root around for chilli gold. And there's all colours and shapes and contours and magnificence. There's smells I can't tell and pungent unctuous wonder that would get me high were I to let it. HIGH indeed. Amongst it all there are people draped and grinning, humbly noble and nobly humble. They're not even selling – just presenting. Te naaa! Ah tingle on that cymbal and bang that drum for it's throbbing now, just throbbing.

This ain't no Romford Market. And I'm not prodding a rainwater slumped tarpaulin cover in order to splash an old lady, not for nothing. Not even a raise on my seven pound a week. Sorry, Charlie boy. No dice, no deal. Not here. For here is like no other place on earth, mate.

But it's not just fruit and vegetables and spices. There's cakey biscuit type things covered in all sorts of colours, rainbowed up and just daring me to partake. And I do. I hand over a note and buy a transparent bag of cookies that could be sweet or salty or sour or anything at all. For a moment I display my wares as my stagger becomes a stroll. For a further moment I feel I'm almost a local. But I'll never be as local as the woman who is stretched out on a counter of fish, her head resting upon an ice bucket and her feet just dripping with sweat and produce. Now that's a local. She sleeps so sweet and barely breathes. Bustle bonanza is all around yet she barely breathes.

"You want?" a man asks.

I shake my head, not sure whether he's enquiring about the fish or the woman.

"I'll be alright," I say.

"Me too!" he replies with a grin.

Ah it's like every colour and every movement is a musical note. This isn't a market it's a symphony. Snapping out of the voluptuous vapour I suddenly get the western urge to buy some trainers. My flippidy flops will be no good against the jungle snakes and the bear sized bugs. So it's to the second floor I go – to the clothes and the shoes and the pearls and the upper echelons of all this magic.

Oh, Charlie Fancourt – you are great, but this is a market!

But what a silent market!

The floor I have just left bore no sound but that of the muffle shuffle of feet and the jingle jangle of coins – no blaring of wares or bargaining bargains, no competition and no desperation – just silent, slightly smiling people, standing proudly amidst the produce of their land, accepting, still and entirely full of grace.

From silence onto silence, up and high above the Sandakan streets now.

I must confess that I've long had a shopping knee. It's been my saviour in supermarkets, shopping centres and assorted shops all around the south of England. I once even managed to convince a girl whom I was with at the time that there was a certain concrete used in the floors of capitalist structures that offended my communist knees. I recall that before I had even finished my (somewhat intricate!) explanation, she had huffed off into consumerland leaving me to dream upon a bench. But here in Sandakan Market, thousands of miles from my Tollesbury home, my shopping knee is energised and cheeky.

I saunterbounce to the repository of trainers. It is as if I have floated. Perhaps I have. I momentarily think that if I can indeed saunterbounce and float, then maybe I require no footwear at all. But then I think of the snakes and the spiders and the spiky and slimy and decide it's just as well to be prepared.

There are two women in the small booth as I approach. There's a wooden wall at the back and one on either side, all full of shelves containing trainers and shoes. One of the women sits on a box towards the rear and another stands shoulders back and smiling at the front. They are like two beautiful figurines on one of those old mechanical clocks who rotate places as the hour turns. I wait to be beckoned in, to be asked if I can be helped, how my day is, but not a word comes forth from the lips of these two images of serenity.

"Hi," I say.

"Hello," says the woman in the front.

"Can I have some trainers, please?"

The woman at the back giggles, bows her head and covers her face with her hands. Her companion manages to stifle a guffaw and instead lifts her right hand, points slowly to first the left wall, then the back wall and then the right wall. Her left hand remains on her hip as if it is an inherent part of her equilibrium during the whole process.

"Ah. OK. Can I just have a pair of size nines, please?"

Now I've foxed her! Not that I meant to. It's just I don't like shopping and I've never been one for fashion.

"But which ones would you like?"

"Any. I don't mind. Just size nines though. I'm eight and a half really but I think if I get nines then if my feet swell in the heat I might still be OK."

"You want that I should choose?"

I nod. Her friend is staring at me like I've just declared I'm about to rob the place.

"Any ones?"

"Yeah. Not pink though."

"Not pink?"

"No."

Moments later a pair of black trainers with a red Nike stripe down the side are being placed gently into a brown paper bag. I hand over some money and with a wonderful sense of accomplishment head towards the stairway that will lead me back down to the streets and to the awaiting Faz and Cheng. It's as I'm about to descend that I hear a rushing of feet behind me. Am I about to be robbed? Ah I hope not, not this early in the trip. Not in a market. I could have stayed in Romford for that.

"Sir! Sir!"

I turn round and see my gorgeous smiling vendor holding up the brown bag containing my new trainers. She hands the bag to me and grins. I offer up a bashful smile and roll my eyes to the ceiling.

"Cheers," I say.

She skips back to her post and I hear beautylaughter in the air as I make my way down to the street. With each step I take I think of how many ways I could have been fleeced and taken advantage of just in the last half an hour. For one who professes full faith in the human race, I still manage to doubt the motives of my fellow people on occasion. Something I'll work on. It's a long old trek this FRUGALITY business…

As I step back out into the sun, I see Cheng's minibus on the other side of the street. I nervously cross the road, still not entirely confident which way I should be looking, holding my trainers in their paper bag in one hand and my bag of biscuit cake things in the other. Faz is out of his passenger seat and opening the door even before I have made the kerb.

"All good? Did you get any pearls?"

"No," I say, clambering in. "Just some trainers and these."

I present the see-through bag of green topped things to him and decide in a moment of pathetic imperialist hegemony to present an offering to my serfs.

"You want one?" I ask. "What are they, anyway?"

Faz takes one and smells it. He looks over at me and then takes the tiniest of bites.

"I have never had these before," he says. "I don't know what they are."

He hands the substantial remainder to Cheng who is just pulling out onto the road. In that moment I fear the car behind is about to ram us into oblivion. Cheng puts his foot on the accelerator, takes a huge mouthful of whatever Faz has handed to him and then spits just as huge a globful of it out the window, almost knocking a startled cyclist off her bike.

"I don't think Cheng is a fan," Faz says, turning to me, smiling.

"Yeah, does look that way." It is from that moment that I consider Faz to be my best friend. There is just something about him that makes me feel OK. "Where to now?" I ask.

"To Puu Jih Shih."

"What's that then?"

"The Buddhist temple."

"Good stuff," I reply.

Faz turns back to face front and I am left once again with my hollowness.

I have no idea when I first heard of Buddha and his thoughts and ideas. It can't have been at Boys' Brigade because that was just port and starboard charging madness, penny chews and losing at football. It can't have been at school. That was all things bright and beautiful and being told by the Religious Education teacher that questions were unChristian. Perhaps it was John Lennon singing that "Karma" was gonna get me *instantly*. He fascinates me but his view of karma does not quite equate with mine. Karma doesn't 'get' – it giggles and moves on. Well that's my experience anyway. Although I do agree with most of "Imagine". Especially the imagine bit. Perhaps it was through Jack Kerouac that I first encountered Buddhist thought? Or was that pints of red wine with ice cubes? Now *that's* gonna get me. Sure as anything.

It's these thoughts I'm thinking as Cheng silently winds the minibus up through the Sandakan hills above Sandakan Bay to the Buddhist temple of Puu Jih Shih.

I look behind me briefly just to get some sort of idea of the steepness of the hill upon which we travel and white figures, statues of ancient men march into my vision, lining the road on each side, striding up this hill, moving yet still, entrancing me and fixing me. And when I languidly face front I am in awe. For as Cheng slows down I see three giant archways before me – one in the centre of the road and one on each flank. They are of white stone and curves so perfect and edges so sharp, held up by blocks that are like ankles, the feet embedded far inside the earth. I wonder for a moment whether these arches are rising from the ground or sinking back into it. And as my gaze is drawn up, up, up, I see the colours on the top front facia, just beneath obtuse oriental roofs that seem to be made of beautiful petals. The roofs tilt up at the edges towards the blue sky, as if the firmament itself is balanced upon this very structure. There are colours I have no words to describe – not peach but almost, cerise but not quite. This is vision in a different dialect, pure and simple.

Cheng drives us through the centre arch and pulls up on the left hand side. Faz opens my door and he and I walk together in silence further up until we reach the temple.

Three more arches face me beneath an overhanging roof that is suspended by colourful pillars that remind me of the crayons I used to have as a child. And that's it, that's it, there is a childlike wonder not just in me but, so it seems, in the creation of this whole temple, colours that any designer or art teacher would never put together, curves against lines and a LOVE that FLOATS. I am above all and within all now. I am a child as I am a man.

"You need to take your shoes off before you go in," Faz says to me as he slips his off and lays them down side by side.

"They're in the van," I reply.

"OK. Then let's go."

Faz smiles at me and were he a woman I do believe he would have taken my hand. Instead he just offers me a wink and ushers me inside. Unlike the POW camp, he follows me in this time. And I do believe he shares my joy, for now I see the reason for the archways.

The polished tiled floor, all terracotta and gleam is cool upon my feet just like I've stepped into refreshing waters after a dusty trek. Taking your shoes off before entering isn't about bringing in the dirt, it's about giving yourself a chance to truly experience every sensation of this place. I struggle to make sense of it all – there is just so much, from the crazy columns and the creatures that swirl around them to the painted ceiling that is ten times Michelangelo.

I turn to Faz and he points out the square tiles on one of the walls.

"Each of these has the name on of a villager that donated to the building of the temple."

There are hundreds of them, thousands maybe. There are bricks at Dagenham & Redbridge FC with the names on of people who have donated money to the building of one of the stands. It's kind of the same thing I guess…

I turn back around and face the focal point of this temple. There are three thrones raised high on a platform. Upon each of these thrones sits a golden, cross-legged figure and upon the head of each is a sort of black hat. The thrones are red and gold at the base with flecks of cyan and between each of the thrones is a smaller golden statue that stands upon a plinth. There is so much to take in for my western eyes. I've been to The Tower of London and looked upon the crown jewels. I've been to Hampton Court and The Victoria and Albert Museum but never have I seen such opulence, such shimmer and such shine. I have no idea what any of it means. Wealth, particularly ostentatious wealth, has ever repulsed me, but this, well this just makes me smile.

I look down at my bare feet and regard my smiling face in the polished floor tiles. I search the temple for answers and happily find none. But what I do find though is a low wooden table of books in one corner. I gaze at the covers and touch them gently with my fingertips. There is a paper sign on the table that states you can take any book you please – donation optional. Faz comes over to me and speaks in a soft voice.

"You going to take one?" he asks.

"Wouldn't seem right," I reply.

"Why not?"

"I don't know. Just not used to getting something for nothing. It would kind of feel like I was nicking it."

"Nicking?"

"Stealing."

Faz grins.

"Should I then?"

"If it feels right, it is right," he replies. "I'll meet you outside," he adds before gliding over towards the archways.

I was once in Stratford-Upon-Avon in search of Shakespeare's grave. Having found the church in which he is buried, I had stepped solemnly inside. Before me was a sign that stated I would have to pay £2 if I wanted to pass through and see his resting place. Having only enough money for a pint, I had left somewhat startled and sad. And now, on the other side of the world, here I am in a Buddhist temple where they are giving away books for nothing – books of life and love and enchantment. Yet still I find myself unable to take one.

Though the air within the temple cools me in a way I adore, I find myself yearning for the outerdoors. Eschewing the front archways, I step out of another archway at the side and gaze across the morass of green treetops that flow down the hillside towards the outskirts of the town and into the blue of Sandakan Bay. There is a darker blue that bestrides the horizon, curving away across my eye line, stretching forth across the world.

When I am high up at times, I have the urge to jump off into the void. This is no exception. I feel myself edging closer and closer to the edge until I am leaning over the white stone balcony. It is Faz who calls me back.

"Time to go," he calls. "Cheng is out front waiting for us."

I nod my head and drag myself away from the precipice. Walking around to the front of the building, I stop suddenly at a sight that rears up to my left. On a patch of hillside bereft of trees there is a large ring of perfectly round bushes and, in the centre, four right-angled lengths of hedge that intersect to form the shape of a Swastika. My mind is instantly filled with the faces of those men who survived the Sandakan Death Marches and with the numbers of those who didn't. I feel a little unsteady and light-headed. A hand upon my shoulder breaks the spell. It's Faz again.

"Cheng has started the engine. He'll go without us if we don't hurry."

I am numb. I feel neither the stones beneath my feet nor the sudden heat of the sun as we step out into the open and head for the van.

"That..." I begin to say.

"Ah that's not what you think," Faz replies. "That's a Buddhist swastika. It is the heart of the Buddha."

"Really?"

"Yes."

Faz makes a quick dash for the van as it is clear that Cheng is pulling away. As he leaps in, I am still a few yards behind. Cheng is laughing as he leans out of the window at me.

"Bye!" he yells. "Bye!"

He stops when he has passed through the arches and he is still laughing when I get in the van. I can see his face in the mirror – there are what looks like tears on his cheeks and his shoulders are still shaking in admiration of his own prank.

"Where are we going now?" I ask, a little out of breath and looking forward to time to think.

"To the batcave!" Faz announces.

The van hurtles down the hill at high speed, its driver roaring with laughter and my guide doing his best to recite the de-ne-ne-ne-na of the *Batman* theme tune.

It is then that I truly see that I have put my life in the hands of these two strangers.

"Trust everybody, for at heart everybody is good." I say to myself with a rueful smile upon my red and sweating face.

To the batcave indeed.

6. Cavernblack Giggleslip

The afternoon eases on and I become drowsy despite the rickety rocking and rolling of Cheng's van as he seems to purposely avoid the small bumps in the road in order to joyfully career into the larger ones. With each jerk and jump, I hear Cheng laugh at the edges of my somnolence, colouring the cloud of sleep that descends upon me from high above.

Ah I need a drink I think as I sink into sleep.

But sleep is never just sleep and dreams are never just dreams. It's whirl and swirl and blur and thunder. That's dreams, whether you like it or not. Sometimes there is sweet sunlight and at other times just pure mercy and dark and breakings and thud. There is no control, never control. In this honky tonk van on the way from Buddha to Batcave all I feel is hoppity. Just movement and that's all. A jaunty hump bedump. There is no theology here, no deep thinkings and wonderment, just honky tonk and be what may. Bring on that batcave, I think as I awake. Bring it all on.

Oh to have a drink in me.

It's all so *fearful*.

We have come to the dimming of the day. It's not yet here but it's getting there.

"Where are we?" I ask.

"Stopping," Faz replies.

We are stopping.

I breathe deep.

And breathe again.

I step weary out of the van and stand aside on the crunch gravel as Faz slides my door shut. Cheng leaps dramatically out from the driver's seat and lands two footed spraying small stones and puffdust into the evening. Within seconds I smell the scent of cigarettes. Cheng has come around to join myself and Faz and the two of them stand smoking in silence, cowboy cool and thoroughly invincible.

There is a dark tinge to the blue of the sky, a depth that makes me wonder that it may be even denser than the land upon which I stand. I tentatively lift up a hand in an attempt to prod the sky, hoping my finger will succeed in sending ripples across the heavens and all around the world and that I will slip into the gravy brown earth without so much as a plip. But I just find myself pointing like a dumb fool at a building I didn't know was there. Well it was a good effort anyhow.

"That's where we need to get our tickets," Faz says helpfully, flicking his spent cigarette into the bushes at the edge of the car park.

Cheng is blowing smoke rings and continues to do so as Faz and I head over towards the small wooden structure that I have so cannily discovered. I can't help but look over my shoulder occasionally and admire Cheng's work. I wonder if he is trying to blow a smoky sailing ship that he may then sail away on. If he's not there when we get back from the batcave, I resolve to search for him forever in the ocean sky.

"Welcome to Gomantong Caves," says the man who gives Faz the tickets. He also hands him a yellow hard hat each for us both.

"Do you want gloves?" Faz asked me.

"What for?"

"Some of the handrails in the cave are, well... You might want some."

"I'll be alright."

And immediately I am brought back to Kenya in September 2008 – my honeymoon.

I'm on the Indian Ocean just off the coast of Mombassa. Everything is flat and blue and still. The boat which at first glance I thought looked modern is in fact almost falling apart at the creaky seams. There are seven of us on the deck aside from the two man crew. Ostensibly we are there to go snorkelling, to look at the fish and to swim around a little. I struggle with swimming. It's not so much the physical movements but the breathing and the whole concept. I can float adequately. Until I sink. But then I need a drink. There's not much drink to be had in the Indian Ocean. I know that now.

"Do you want a life jacket?" the sailor asks me.

"What for?"

"Some of the waves in the sea are, well... You might want one."

"I'll be alright."

The sailor went around the group as we all bobbed up and down beneath the hot sun. All my fellow bobbers accepted a life jacket. The fact they were pink reinforced to me that my decision had been fine.

Me in a pink life jacket? I can't swim very well but I'll still look coolity cool!

Moments later I'm flapping around in the depths all desperate and puffing like a snorter. The sailor comes to my rescue though, throwing a red and white hard rubber ring towards me. He yells at me to grab hold whilst he in turn holds onto the worn rope attached to the ring. And thus does he tow me around the ocean for half an hour so

I can look at the bright little fishes without struggling to breathe.

Coolity cool.

Coolity cool.

"Gomantong Caves?" I say to Faz as I follow him across a narrow slatted bridge towards the trees. "Is it named after the man who discovered them?"

"Probably," he replies.

Once we are through the dense green trees, we step into a clearing that feels like it is only just above water. There is a large pond in front of a stilted wooden structure and around it are reeds and rushes and long grass. As I follow Faz across it to the cave on the other side of the pond it feels like I am walking not on earth but upon knotted grass and dead vegetation, as if this is some kind of floating island. I look back over at the pond as we cross the bridge that leads directly into the cave and somehow expect the me of a few years back to pop up in the middle of it, life jacket and all, breathing at last and urging me to go back and get some pink gloves.

It's the smell that first gets me. Acrid isn't the word. It's close but it's not the word. At first I'm repulsed and then I'm drawn. It reminds me of when I used to empty bins for the council when I was twenty-one. There was something *reassuring* about certain smells that oozed from the black bags back then, something I could relate to. And it's the same now. There's a familiarity of sorts, a sense of degradation, of impeccable imbalance.

"That's bat shit," Faz tells me.

"What is?"

"That smell. Bat shit."

He puts his gloves on and urges me not to touch the handrails.

I know people talk about caves having mouths, but this one, this Gomantong Cave truly has. There are no lips, no lush, no drips, just sparse railings for teeth and a raggedy straggedy green moustache that dangles down into the blackness from above, eschewed by the hillside and neglected by wind and by rain and by sun and by me. You just have to go in to see more. You just have to. So I do.

And without taking a step I'm in. I've been sucked and swallowed and my eyes are closed. When I open them there is light over my shoulder, the light of the outerdoors, but before me, in the cave, the huge cave that wells up around me like a yawn, there are sights I never have seen before.

The first thing I notice are the ladders that drop down from the roof of the cave to a few feet from the floor. I climb them with my eyes until I see rope bridges that cross the heights in darkness and trepidity trepidity. They waver before my fallen vision.

"Do men fall?" I ask Faz, expecting him to say 'Probably.'

"Not anymore," he says instead.

"Wow," I say to myself and inadvertently inhale a gulpful of gwomph.

Ah the smell and the *feel* of the place.

I feel like I'm in the middle of a Heath Robinson sketch from the middle ages. No cogs here, just fibre and brush and shadow and doomy drip echoes.

"We'll go up this way," Faz says. "Then we can walk up to the end and come back around."

He scribes a horseshoe shape in the dank air and I nod and follow, holding onto the metal handrail that curves up and to the left of me. Immediately I am repulsed at the crack of cockroach beneath my knuckles. I wince at the thought that I may have been wearing pink gloves and move on, all man-like and conquering.

So I proceed to follow Faz as he steps up the dark stone slope into the centre of the cave. The entire place is silent to my western ears. It is as if my ability to hear has been nullified and my vision and smell enhanced, for in this quiet gloom space I spy insects and drip drops and fade and white shards of sleek. It's a short distance but a slow climb. With no light but that which stands bold at the cave entrance, the cockroaches that abound all orange brown are like stickers in a sticker book, erratically placed by a five year old hand whose joy is not in the precision but in the placing.

I recoil from a Tupperware lunch box that sits neatly on a hewn edge in the cave wall to my right. A dozen or more cockroaches scratch dolefully upon the lid. I don't know whether they are trying to get in or whether they are delighting in the fact they have made their way out. Faz turns to look at me to make sure I'm still here. I'm glad he is leading me, so glad.

"Look at this," he calls back to me.

I stumble through the dark to where Faz stands, just at the apex of the horseshoe curve of our route. Before me, on the ground, there are two thin dirty mattresses in colours that exist only outside of my experience – for I haven't been where they have been, not even close. I once slept on the platform at Barking Station and I confess to having spent the night in the odd park and on more than a few floors but this, this is in a different universe. Where we are is high up in the cave. Below us, perhaps fifty feet down is the pit floor of the cave. And resting on a precarious edge are these two mattresses, side by side like slain lovers on the shore.

"What's that about?" I ask Faz.

He just looks up to the pin point tip of the inner cave. I follow his eye-line and discern movement, just.

"You see those two?"

"Are they people?"

"Yes."

"Up there on that ladder?"

"Yes."

I wow again. I think I'm beginning to see where Cheng gets his wowing from.

"Well," Faz continues. "They're the ones who get the bird nests, the real experts. They only have to work a couple of months a year they get paid so much. Bird's Nest Soup is a delicacy in China. The Chinese love it. Those two men collect the nests in the most dangerous part of the cave."

"And they sleep here too?"

"Yes."

"For two months?"

"Probably."

There's cockroaches at Barking Station but most of them wear suits. This is a different thing entirely. Well almost entirely. I wonder if there is a hierarchy amongst cockroaches the same as there is amongst station roaches and think perhaps there is. I don't have time to consider my thesis in depth however for Faz now takes me by the arm.

"Be careful on your way down," he says. "It's easy to fall."

I am pondering the wisdom of his statement when I slip and realise he is talking about the slip slidiness of the black stone floor as opposed to offering me a nugget of Christmas cracker wisdom.

"You OK?"

I blink back a tear and smile mightily.

"Just a flesh wound," I reply.

It is as if we are not even there. The men carry on regardless, doing the work they have done for centuries, these days harnessed but still so high up as to make me feel tiny. I look up into the heights of this black cave – Simud Hitam is its name. The ceiling is almost a hundred metres high and at the very peak of it there are men gently removing swiftlet nests made of feathers and saliva in order that they can be gathered, cleaned and sold for Bird's Nest Soup, that ancient delicacy that has been on the Chinese menu for almost five hundred years. The nests can sell for anything up to two and a half thousand dollars a piece.

"Close your mouth," Faz says to me.

I turn to look at him, unaware that my mouth is even open.

"Why?"

"Cockroaches."

He winks at me and smiles before leading me out from the black of the dark into the white of the light.

>The white of the light
>and there are dogs
>three small dogs in the arms of man
>three shiny small black dogs
>in the arms of man.

Under the arms of man and then hurled into the pool of water that stands stank stark and unrippling before the wooden house I saw before I entered the cave. And those dogs laugh! They do! And if they could they would have gathered themselves back into the arms of man only to be thrown in again. But they don't. Because they can't. And we move on back to the van – the cave and the giggling dogs nothing but a slip in time in my carnivorous cavernblack giggleslip of a mind.

> The black of the light
> and there are bats.

"And there are bats," says Faz as we reach the car park and the van once more.

"I thought that was it."

"He thought that was it," Faz says to Cheng who closes up his laptop. Something western superior inside of me wonders why Cheng has a laptop.

"The bats?" Cheng replies.

Faz nods.

Cheng grins and opens his laptop back up before going to sit on the grassy hill behind us.

Bemused but smiling I look across at Faz who bids me follow him. We go up the hill, leaving Cheng on the lower slope and get to a point about thirty feet up from the ground. I see the cave from which we've just come and above it another cave. Faz tells me the higher one is where the really valuable birds' nests are found – the white swiftlet nests. The public aren't allowed near it and it is twice as big as the one that awed me. Above to the left there are tall trees that climb up to the sky so fast it's as if they are standing still.

> Green and shadows
> dark and fading light.
> Green to black
> and back again
> blue in the middle
> and yellow on the tinges.

Between the branches of a big old tree in the big old distance there is an wonderful sight in silhouette. I can't describe it. Not even after a skinful. So I'll just tell you. It's a female orang-utan and its baby. I know that because Faz pointed them out to me. I thought they were just strange branches on a strange tree. Shows what I know. Nothing.

But I'm open to magic and to majesty and to magicians so I am able to follow his finger where it points.

But my guide's finger then sways to the right and up, up, up and I follow with all my soul. My eyes are way behind, just as they should be, way, way behind. Blinking's for fools. Souling is clear water beautiful. I recommend souling like I recommend my mates. My drink sodden golden hearted banter beauty friends who unknown to all but me place the planets in their orbit and the waves in the waves. That's what I'm thinking as I follow Faz's finger to the skies.

"There's the bats," says Faz. "The dots in the sky."

He retreats as if the effort is too much for him, as if he has produced every tiny bat from its blurry wholesome blackbat glory.

For above me in the sky so blue are puffs of bats a million strong, a yawn from the cave that forms a wavering bubble of dotness that floats into the ever distance like nothing I have ever seen before. Then just as it fades into light so another appears – broad and wonderful, pulsing and dit dot perfect, bats being bats and this earth utter perfection. This goes on for an hour and more. Bats in the sky in befuddled huddles edging into the night and disappearing into the night. And more and more and more. Yawn and waft and pulse and throb sensational. I'm gone. I'm gone I'm truly gone.

"Ready to go?" asks Faz.

"I reckon," I say.

So go we do – back to the van, Cheng in his driver seat with his laptop stowed away, Faz in front and me laid out behind weary and worn, just wondering and wondering.

We drive for hours and finally come to a stop in the darkness. I let myself be taken from the van to a small boat that drifts silent in the blackness of the Borneo night towards a riverbank of which I have no knowledge. A young boy steers. Cheng is beside him, his eyes shining. I am in the back with Faz, barely awake. I don't know what is happening to me. I am beginning to lose who I am, who I thought I was. But that's OK. It's alright really. For I am nothing if not hopeful, full of FRUGALITY and ready, if necessary, to meet my jungle maker.

7. Bread on the Water Now

Did I dream the lapping slap schlop of the water against the wooden boat, the faraway stars reflected in the dull green of the river, the black trees, the shadows and the silhouettes? Were those four short women, all smiles and bare feet, real who served me with rice and other delights the moment my weary body sagged from the boat onto the wooden decking, enlivening me enough just so I could pad my way to the room in which I now find myself?

I guess it all happened – as much as anything happens. I ache in a wonderful way. It's a new day, a new adventure, the continuing rolling of my strange life on the plains of this earth.

I open my eyes and spy a pink pygmy elephant. I open them wider and see it is a photo on the wall next to a large dripping window through which I can see dense green foliage. I look from the photo to the window and back again just to see which one will be the first to provide evidence of its reality. Neither moves. Then they both do, just slightly. A drenched slender leaf wavers. The pink pygmy elephant flicks his tail gently. I rub my eyes and realise that nothing matters. It's all movement and movement is good. I step out of bed and into my shorts, put on the t-shirt I have evidently thrown on the floor the night before, pat my pink pygmy elephant between his ears (he smiles and winks at me) and head out of the room like I'm stepping into a film.

Once out into the early morning of the day I look right and see up ahead, at the end of the narrow wooden planked bridge upon which I stand, the same roofed decking from my dream. It's like the one at the place where I had stayed the night before but much smaller. I walk lightly towards it trying to take in everything with all my senses. Either side (I am about ten feet from the ground) there are plants the like of which I have never seen before. Now I am in no way an expert in botany but these things look like they have leapt direct from a fantasy mind! What once would have been a frown upon my forehead is now a smile upon my face. I am beginning to learn I think.

On reaching the decking I see a sign that informs visitors to remove their shoes before entering. I bend down to obey and realise I am not wearing anything on my feet at all.

I hope my pink pygmy elephant friend is OK. I consider bringing him back some breakfast but then wonder what he would like to eat. I'll have to ask him later. If he's still there. Perhaps he's worrying about me? He really shouldn't. I'll be just fine.

"Hi."

It's Faz, sitting at one of the wooden tables, grinning as if he's been waiting for me all his life.

"Hi," I reply before sitting down opposite.

"Did you sleep well?"

I nod. "What time is it?"

Faz checks his mobile phone. "Breakfast time."

I manage to glimpse a photo on his phone of Faz with his arm across the shoulders of a beautiful blonde woman. I'm not sure he notices that I have seen her. He seems far too excited (in a cool way!) at the idea of what the four short ladies are about to serve us.

"Is it just us here?" I ask.

"At the moment. Cheng is around and Nelson and his family. I think there might be one or two more parties coming over the next couple of days. The reports of the troubles have really hit us all hard. That's why it's so great you're here."

"Who is Nelson?"

"Ah, you'll meet him. This whole place is his."

"Are those women his wives?" I whisper as the bare foot ladies recede back into the shadows having deposited bowls of wonder before us.

Faz chuckles. "Yes. Nelson has four wives. One for every day of the week."

"Really?"

"Yes. We only have four day weeks here in Borneo. It's a tradition. In Borneo years I am sixty-one years old."

Open-mouthed I stare at him.

Before I can close my mouth, Cheng thuds in and sits down with us. He looks at me and then at Faz.

"Morning!" he declares. I think that's what he says anyway. His mouth is so full of food I wonder if he has walked in with it already there or whether he has somehow swiped it without either myself or Faz noticing.

"I was just telling our friend about Nelson's four wives," Faz says to Cheng.

Cheng nods and some rice comes out of one of his nostrils and splats onto the table. He proceeds to flick it on the floor Subbuteo style and carries on munching.

"Four day week here!" he says to me, grinning, rice tumbling from between his lips like tiny white lemmings.

I see I'm being played for a fool and grin. What else can I do? I tuck into the glorious food and we three clear all the bowls until all that is left is the rising sun upon the river and a satisfaction I have rarely felt before.

"This morning," says Faz, "we will be going on a jungle walk across the other side of the river. Nelson has some leech socks and boots for us. One of Nelson's boys will be our captain on the boat. Then I will be your jungle guide on the other side."

"Was that one of Nelson's boys who brought us over on the boat last night?"

"Yes. Nelson's eldest."

Cheng has by now produced his laptop from nowhere and is intent upon it, eyes fixed on the screen, unmoving except for a stubby finger that taps a key rhythmically. It's like he's counting his breaths or something. Or perhaps he's counting mine? I try to slow down my breathing but struggle to see as to whether the rhythm of Cheng's tapping slows with it. I regain my composure and try to erase Cheng's fingers from my thoughts.

"When is the jungle walk?" I ask Faz.

"Just about now," he says, rising. "Follow me and we'll get our leech socks and boots."

Cheng seems not even to have noticed we have left the table.

Leech socks. Until this moment I had never heard of such a thing. I have heard about leeches – mainly in relation to olden day methods of healthcare – but I have no idea what they look like. But these leech socks that Faz throws over to me, they are a tan colour and come up to my knees. You have to wear them over your trousers (which I rush back to put on – my pink pygmy elephant handing them to me and bidding me farewell) and tie them up tightly at the top. I then find myself a pair of wellington boots from a line of perhaps ten pairs and I'm ready for the jungle trek. Faz hasn't put on either the leech socks or boots. I guess he knows what the leeches look like. I wonder if I'm being had again, but I do indeed feel well protected. There's no way I want another Kenya rubber-ring fiasco...

I blow a slow-motion kiss to my pink pygmy elephant and follow Faz back up towards the decking and through to the riverbank where several boats are moored. Sitting in one of them is the dark-haired boy who brought us over the previous night. I see in the light that he is probably about sixteen. He has confident eyes and a way about him that makes me feel instantly safe. I feel he can handle anything, that he is kind and assured and entirely at ease with whatever he does. That being said, I almost fall into the river as I step into the boat. I notice him smile but he tries to hide it beneath his adolescent moustache.

We're on the water now. The netherworld water. I'm floating on this earth. It's six in the morning and I'm not bleary-eyed drunk wondering how I'm going to get into work. I'm aroused and wondering where the crocodiles are.

"Where are the crocodiles?" I ask.

"Asleep," says Faz. "But you need to watch out for the logodiles."

"Logodiles?"

"Logodile!!!" shouts Faz and throws himself forward onto the wooden floor of the small boat. I do the same and close my eyes instinctively. When I open them, Faz is back sitting where he was at the rear of the boat, pointing and smiling. "Logodile," he says again, this time in a whisper.

I follow his finger and see a large, gnarled branch floating in the river. *Fucker* I think to myself. *Fucker*.

Faz's smile turns into the white yellow sun and the river reflects the reflections of the white river sun. Everything splash merges with the flow in the same way as my little pink pygmy elephant winks at me. Form shudders and shakes and dissolves. There is just sunlight, pure sunlight. It's the white of Mick Jagger's shirt in the concert in the park and the white of John Lennon's white room. It is the bright of Thomas Paine's surge and the bright of William Blake's vision. All we have is sun and light and vision and surge. Shadow is a side-effect. Misery is a disease. Wow is wow is wow is wow.

>   We are bread on the water
>   bread on the water now
>   just bread on the water
>   now.

As the sky brightens, the trees on the riverbank loosen their grip on the horizon. There's a swaying now, a cool swaying that serves to gently separate the static from the vibrant. I can almost hear the sound of breaking free, the stretch yawn coming to life of a jungle that knows no time and is entirely unhindered. All around me, all about me, the natural nature loving goodness of all that is wonder sits up, chuckles and strolls down the stroll riverbank – not quite jolly, for there's nothing cool in jolly – at ease, if you please, kind sir. Just. At. Ease.

Everything else is blown away.

At last.

There's no grief here on the river, no screech, no shout, no sulk and no pout. The only danger I can see is from the crafty logodile. And that's not so bad. Especially when I consider where I have been and where I have to go back to. If I could only dispense with this fear of letting go.

There's a thud and a jolt as the boat nudges against the bank on the further side of the river.

Faz hops out and extends a hand towards me. I say I'll be OK and disembark with the same lack of grace with which I had taken my seat just twenty minutes before. Nelson's son steers the boat back across the river as the early morning mist kisscuddles the blueing sky. And there is just me and Faz at the edge of the Borneo jungle on this earthly morn.

>   Down
>   in
>   jun
>   gle
>   land

Faz bends down and tightens my leech socks. I stand upright as if I am merely having my sense of balance adjusted.

"Just follow me," says Faz. "Try not to touch anything. Just in case."

The bank rises steeply and then the gradient gets slightly easier as we enter the canopy of the trees. As the ground levels out, so my eyes are cast upwards, ever upwards, as if I'm never satisfied.

And everything is on its side and upside down. Straight green leaves point pointy all spiralled and rotated, spurting out from magician sleeve branches – pow and whoosh and there they are. But it doesn't take me long to focus out and focus in to the spaces between the darkness. For it's sky I seek and I'm heaven bound. Blue is white and white is blue and there's a pattern wherever you look. There's nothing going around but my eyes. The earth is static. It wouldn't at all surprise me if it were flat. What does it matter anyhow? It's only dreams and visions, majestic as they are. Keep your facts away from me, I don't need them anymore. You can call me anything you like, even Al.

"Are you alright?" Faz asks.

"Yep."

"Let's go then."

I follow Faz up to the level. Heat is hot heat. Everything is sharpened and heightened. I'm doing my best to follow my guide on this jungle path but I'm drawn, *so drawn*, to all that is either side, below and above me. And I begin to wonder as my steps turn to a drawl and a trudge whether it is me moving at all or whether it is the succulent growth and earthy wonder that moves. I stand still for a moment and catch a sapling half in motion. I wink at it and it shudders. I do not move for fully thirty seconds. Neither does the jungle. But I blink first and place one foot in front of the other and there we are back again in a semblance of reality. It's a big old game this jungle walk. How can any of this be really happening to a scruffy lad from Dagenham? Part of me thinks I'm still on the plane. But how did I ever get on a plane? Perhaps I'm still eleven years old and sleeping on my desk in double History whilst Mr. Ferguson shakes his head in my general direction. He was great, Mr. Ferguson – probably younger then than I am now.

"Are they mushrooms?" I ask Faz, bending at the knees all tracker style and pointing to some brown white fungal muffins that are sprouting from the base of a tree.

"Probably."

I must confess I'm more Grizzly Madams than Grizzly Adams but I'm pretty sure they are probably mushrooms.

We walk and we walk and there is a pulsing in the air. It's like the fingers of a madman are hovering over the black and white keys of a jungle green piano, just holding off from touching those keys, throb hovering in a heartbeat fashion. Just throb hovering. In a heartbeat fashion.

Underneath the stars I'll meet you. For I love you.

We walk for an hour or so through the hot and the heat and the air and the drench until I feel I am merging with the hot and the heat and the air and the drench. It's like I have become vapour and droplet – a magical mystical womp of buzz baloomph.

And then there is the river once more.

The sun is high now and I am warming to this fragrance. On this morning.

Faz leads me down to what looks like some kind of jetty – wooden planks upon struts that jut out some twenty feet across the river. It's like a landing stage. Whatever a landing stage is.

"Nelson's son will pick us up from here in about thirty minutes," says Faz.

The sun is grand now, hot upon me as I sit upon these warming boards. Faz rolls his trouser legs up to his knees and sits on the edge, dangling his thin brown legs into the water, the gentle lapping teasing his calves.

"This is good," he says.

I smile at him and agree, with no intention of doing anything other than lying on my back on the wood and dozing a little.

"They don't eat you," says Faz.

"What don't?"

"The small fish that are eating me."

"What do you mean?"

"Roll up your trousers and see. You can take off your leech socks. You're safe from them now."

I do as he says. For he is Buddha. One of them anyway. I am Buddha too. I just didn't realise it back then.

I sit next to Faz and, all courage me, ease my feet into the river. Within seconds there's a nudging and a nibbling about my toes and *between* my toes. Immediately I lift my feet from out of the water and roll onto my side on the wooden platform.

"Logodile?" Faz asks.

I regain my cool and check my feet for damage. If anything, they are cleaner than before and just a little bit pinky.

"They're just little fish," says Faz.

"You know what. I think this is what people pay for in London. Loads of these little fish in buckets or something and you put your feet or hands in there and it's some kind of health thing."

"People pay for this?"

"Yeah. Kind of a posh thing."

Faz shakes his head and smiles.

"All free here," he says, turning his palms to the sky. He lights a cigarette and sits there with his feet in the fish nibble river, his eyes closed, the glow from the tip of his cigarette and the smoke he inhales the only signs that he is even breathing at all.

I turn back to the water and stare at it, wondering how safe it would be to once again put my feet in it. Bravery has never been my strongest suit so I decide to lie on my front and put my hand in, just the tips of my fingers first. The water ripples in gentle circles, the high sun shimmer glimmering on the expanding pools. Within moments a hoard of wriggle black nibble fish appear, like iron filings to a magnet. I withdraw my hand just as they reach me and turn to Faz, a silly grin upon my face.

"Stay still," Faz says coolly. "You have a leech on your neck."

I don't move. I barely breathe.

Faz leans over to me and plucks the leech from my skin. I didn't feel it upon me and I didn't feel its release. I watch the small red creature twist and turn between Faz's thumb and forefinger and then I touch the side of my neck. There is blood upon my fingers where the leech had been plucked mid-suck.

"Here. This will sort it out. Give me your hand."

Faz then proceeds to tap ash from the end of his almost spent cigarette into my palm.

"Just put that on the wound. It will dry it out and heal it."

"Really?"

"Yes."

I do and it does.

"Where is the leech now?" I ask. "I thought they were bigger than that."

"I've eaten it. Fresh leech is a delicacy. English blood is my favourite. It's not as bitter as Welsh blood and less sour than Scottish."

"I have so much to learn," I say.

Half an hour later, Nelson's son arrives with the boat. I step in and Faz follows, sitting up front behind our silent companion. Though the sights about me on the quiet river are serene, it is the rise and fall of Faz's shoulders that draw my eye. I do believe he is giggling.

8. Smoking a Pipe in the Rain

By the time we have reached the other side of the river and I have stepped once more onto the land, the clouds have gathered. The once blue sky has gone from union blue to confederate grey in a matter of moments. And then the rain does fall. Faz leaps by me, kicks off his shoes and stands by the table where I met him just a few hours ago. Nelson's son ties up the boat and moves like a ballerina. Either the rain doesn't bother him or he is but a raindrop himself. He has mastered the art of stopping – in so many ways.

Nelson's four ladies spray and spread out from the side door at the far end of the platform as if the whole wooden structure has just been fizz shaken up by an unseen hand. They set about pulling various cords that dangle from the roof, releasing tarpaulins that whoosh thwomp down to create olive green shadow walls. The increasingly heavy rain rattles deep upon the tarpaulins and they bow inwards at times to its magnificence.

The rain has long been my favourite weather, so I couldn't pass up this riversurge drench, skulking beneath a grand canopy. I pad in my bare feet over to one of the tarpaulins that flap hang between the decking and the riverbank. I pull it to one side a little and peek through. And thus do I see the Water Monitor Lizard.

He is about six feet in length and looks to be made of black and white chain mail. His long sturdy body and daring flat tail are like giants to his little girl arms and legs. But I'm not going to tell him that. Not with his jaw. Not with his teeth. He is lying on the bank, straight and still, puffing upon a pipe. Perhaps when you live your life in the water, a downpour is something of a relief. It doesn't take me long to realise he is reciprocating my stare.

"And you are?" he asks me, his voice much higher pitched than I expect.

"Sorry. Just watching the river."

The Water Monitor Lizard blinks heavily and I swear I hear him sigh.

"Yes. I am. Watching the river. It's what I do."

"What are you looking for?"

"Everything and nothing. That way, I am never disappointed."

"Right."

"Yes I am. Right."

"Is that why you're called a Water Monitor Lizard? Because you monitor the water?"

He nods. And then I wonder how he did that. For it's not easy to nod whilst you're smoking a pipe in the rain.

I leave the Water Monitor Lizard to his pipe and his rain and return to sit down opposite Faz, who is looking at some photos on his phone.

"There's a big Water Monitor Lizard out there," I say.

"He took all my money off me at cards a few months ago," Faz replies, not looking up. "More of a shark than a lizard he is sometimes."

I consider this for a moment and wonder at the fact I am sober. Very sober. More sober than I have been in years. Yet I have just had a conversation with a six foot lizard in the Borneo rain. Wonderful! Still, I could murder a tiny can of Tiger beer.

"Tiny can of Tiger beer?" Faz asks me before wandering over to a hatch in the wall and returning with two small blue and yellow cans.

Over the next few minutes, Faz and I down our tiny cans of Tiger beer. One of Nelson's ladies takes our empties the moment they are drained and replaces them with fresh cold ones. And so we get down to business.

"So how long you been doing this, Faz?"

"Doing what?"

"This tourist guide thing. You know, taking people like me around."

"Six years with this company. Two with the one before."

"How old are you? I thought you were only about twenty or something."

Faz grins and looks even younger.

"I'm twenty-seven. How old are you?"

"Forty-three."

"When I first saw you I thought you were my age. Then sometimes I look at you and you look like a hundred. Forty-three is a good average."

"It is in cricket. I'd be happy with that average."

"I know of cricket. We don't play it here. It's big in Australia."

"My favourite sport. I love football, but I *really* love cricket."

"It's good to love."

I nod in appreciation and close my eyes for a moment. When I open them, another tiny can of Tiger beer has appeared.

"Do you live near Liverpool?" Faz asks me, all expectant, suddenly nine years old instead of twenty-seven.

"About two hundred miles away. I'm in Tollesbury, little village in Essex. Southeast of London. How come?"

"They're my team. Liverpool. I've got the shirt. Two shirts. Me and my friends watch all the live Premier League games. And when Liverpool play we all wear our shirts."

"Do you go to the pub and watch it?"

"We don't really have pubs here. There are some in Kota Kinabalu I think. Well places you can drink anyway. I don't know if they show the football."

"What's the football like over here?"

"It's basic. We've only got fourteen teams. Sabah FA are the local team. We got relegated last year. So did our main rivals – Sarawak FA."

"My team are Dagenham & Redbridge."

"You support two teams?"

"No. Same one. Just one team. Dagenham merged with Redbridge Forest back in 1992. Been a Daggers fan since I was eleven."

"Tiny can of Tiger beer?"

"Don't mind if I do,"

The rain keeps falling, rain keeps falling, down, down. I hope my Water Monitor Lizard friend (for I'm sure he is at least that!) is faring well beneath the downpour. The thrapping of the rain upon the tarpaulins and the roof sounds to me like Gene Kruppa jazz drummer thrapping on his drums all groove mcgroove in the fifties New York glow bedazzle night. Buddy Rich didn't come close, mate. Not in my eyes. For you had the madness and had it tight. I puff a pipe to you from here in Borneo, Gene Kruppa. And bemoan the lack of whisky bedoolies.

"Do they have any whisky here?" I ask Faz, trying my best not to sound ungrateful for the tiny cans of Tiger beer.

"Sorry. No. I could take you to some of the villages. There they make Lihing which is rice wine. It's very beautiful. I like it very much. It's not part of the tour though."

"What's it like, the Lihing?"

"It's like beating Everton."

I smile a big smile of rye regret and then wonder what I'm even doing being out here in all this majestic wonder and still considering drinking myself into oblivion.

> Tiny cans of Tiger beer tumble…
> …and tumble.
> But this time I don't mumble
> into my beer.
> I'm loud and clear
> as evening falls
> …as evening
> falls.

"Faz, mate. Is this what you've always wanted to do? This tour guide thing?"

Faz, looking down at the table between us, lifts up his eyes to meet mine divine.

"I have never been anywhere else except Borneo."

"Nowhere?"

"No. It has never occurred to me."

By now, the rain has stopped and the tarpaulins raised like mainsails on this stationary ship that Nelson sails. My Water Monitor Lizard friend has clocked off for the day, put out his pipe and sought the depths.

"I can't believe I'm here," I muse.

"Neither can I. Your government has told you not to come yet you still come. This has been a terrible time for our tourist industry. As you have seen, there is no trouble here. The worst that happens is when the Water Monitor Lizard runs out of tobacco."

"What do you do then, when he runs out of tobacco?"

"Nelson tells him tales of long ago. He likes tales of long ago. The Water Monitor Lizard is very old you see."

"Will you do this forever?"

"Have you had enough?"

"I mean be a tour guide."

"One day I want to own my own company and send people like me to show people like you around Borneo."

"What about Cheng?"

"No-one tells Cheng what to do."

"No-one?"

"Not even his wife."

"Cheng has a wife?"

Faz grins.

"Oh yes," he says. "You'll meet her the day after tomorrow."

"On Turtle Island?"

"Where else?"

Faz and I talk for what seems like hours. The sun sinks ever so slowly here, clinging as it does to the Borneo sky like a dangle bulb in majestic bedsit heaven, making silhouettes of the trees along the river, making gods of you and me.

Cheng and Nelson's son are already in the boat when I stagger step on board. Faz follows me as addled up as I and the four of us head off into the dusk, the only sound that of the water gulping and slapping against the curved planks of our low wooden boat.

It's a slow riding tunnel of love whose roof is the sky and whose sides are the trees.

Faz and Cheng look up and around whilst Nelson's son steers us, the dull throb of the engine rumble-growling at his touch.

"Look," Faz says to me in an urgent whisper. I squint to see where he is pointing, high, high in the branches of a tree.

I don't know if it is a case of my eyes needing to be attuned to the evening light or maybe they have been infected surreptitiously by that western desire to deny wonder.

"I can't see anything. Just the trees."

"Breathe slower. Then you will see."

And I do.

How I missed it the first time, I have no idea. For now, as clear as the image on a postcard is the most curious monkey I have ever seen. I recognise it from the placards at Sandakan Airport. He is sitting in the crevice of a tree, where a branch that must be sturdier than it looks serves as his porchswing riverside seat. He leans back against the trunk, a posture that serves to give greater prominence to his huge round rust coloured belly. One long grey arm is held aloft – I think initially to greet me, but looking closer he is gripping the leaves above. The other arm he rests languidly over a bent knee. He sits in a lotus position, his feet touching one another. I breathe slower still and his face comes into view – a face that is dominated by a huge reddish nose that starts three quarters up his face and finishes just below a thin black mouth. Either side of the nose are two small black eyes that seem too close together. I wonder whether evolution has led to a long ago single black eye being separated by the growing nose. The upper part of the forehead juts out a little casting a shadow over the eyes. He is magnificent – as big as Faz were he to stand I should think and as heavy as all of us in this boat combined.

"That Dutch Monkey," Cheng says, turning to me with a grin.

Cheng has barely uttered more than a few sentences in the days I have known him so his interjection comes as something of a surprise, drawing me away momentarily from the sight I have seen in the tree.

"Isn't it a Proboscis Monkey?" I ask.

"Yes. But also Dutch Monkey. Dutch people very ugly!"

Cheng laughs so intensely at his own joke that he almost laughs himself into the river. Faz smiles and Nelson's son chugs us along.

The sun pauses just for me, just for us, as we are carried along the river. I spot something incredible on the toppest branch of the tallest tree. I am barely breathing at all when my eyes happen upon it. Strangely, it is the white tail with its black marking that I see first as it hangs down beneath the tiny branch upon which its tiny talons grip. Moving up the black body to the head, any breath I had just leaves me. Its beak consists of two downward curving tusk-like protrusions almost as long as its body. Atop that though is an upward curving bright yellow horn that it wears proudly through the dives and the dancehalls. I'm not great with birds (now, now!) but recognise it immediately as a Rhinocer8os Hornbill. It's a privilege to see. And I promise not to make it cry or to ruin its life or to say yes were she to ask me to marry her.

We travel down the river so slow and groovy. The sun embers wink at me as we turn to go back and the colour of the trees fades to black making silhouettes out of all those it touches – the ring-tailed macaques, the proboscis and the hornbills and all those that see this place as their home. When the sun goes down here, it truly goes down. Nelson's son says something to Faz and Faz tells me that we have to moor the boat where we are right now – in a place I don't recognise at all as being near the wooden platforms of our jungle abode.

"It's too dangerous to go on along the river when it's this dark," Faz tells me once we have made the bank. "Don't worry though. This is all part of the experience. Night-time jungle walk time!"

Nelson's son hands out small torches to all of us. It is only when I have turned mine on that I realise how completely black everything has become. I'm breathing fast now. I can't stop myself. I can feel my eyes widen, but they do not aid my vision. And it suddenly hits me that I am alone in the darkness with three strangers who hold my life in their hands. Who will find my body out here? What's to stop them from robbing me and throwing my flaccid body into the deep and gloomy river? Is this how it all ends?

"Just follow my beam," says Faz, closer to me than I thought he was. "We're not far from the lodge. It will feel longer because of the darkness." There is silence. "Like sleep," he adds. "Just like sleep."

His words meld into the nocturne of whisperings and hoot maloot singsong shrills that comprise this Borneo night. There's not a lectern in sight. For tonight is not a night for mere words.

"Oh, and don't look back." Faz whispers. "Never look back."

You can never look back
You can never look back
I never will forget this night.
I wonder if it's a dream
The poise of Summer
The poise of Summer

And, of course, I look back. Behind me is the stone wall of a multi-storey car park in Romford. I'm on the inside, fourth level. I've swept the other three. Just this one to go. *Start at the top and work your way down*, my Paul Michael Glaser lookalike compadre said to me. *That way you know with each step you're nearing home.* I hear the breaking of glass and a bang. It's seven in the evening on a winter's night. It's just me alone in this place that during daytimes is always so full with people and cars and *motion.* Now it's just me and this fear and this blackness. Oh for Faz back then. Oh for Faz back then.

The three torch beams ahead of me are wayward haphazard. I shine my own at my feet just to make sure I'm not about to fall or tread on something that might kill me. Whenever I look up or behind it is as if I am blind. Slowing down my breathing is impossible, so don't give me that one.

All movement stops. There is no shuffle or shoofle of feet, no brush of branch and no twiggle of twig, no breath and no heartbeat. But there are six lights now. Three clicks and there are three lights gone. Faz takes my torch from my hand and switches it off. Just two lights, round and perfect, three feet from me. Even the jungle has quietened, stopped breathing almost just to take a closer look.

As I stare, the white circles of light gain colour and form and I see that they are the eyes of the Western Tarsier. The outer circle is of perfect juice orange, tang magnificence, so circly round. Then next comes the earth, nourished and nourishing, flourishing flourished. And the centre? Well that is just this whole black universe, starry and churning ever moving but still so still. A hint of white shimmers in the very middle of it all and I know it can only be love and love only.

He clings to a tree this Western Tarsier, his long fingers and toes doing what they can to stop him from toppling over. But what am I thinking? He is as steady as the tree itself. It is I who am struggling to maintain my balance. He is no bigger than a few inches yet his eyes contain the past, present and future of my very existence.

I am not real. I do not exist. I know that now.

Later that evening, me and my pygmy elephant are playing chess in my room when he asks me how my day has been.

"How has your day been?" he asks as he takes one of my bishops and puts me into check.

"Extraordinary," I reply, looking up at him.

I try to defend my King with a lone castle.

"Have you ever been beaten at chess by a pygmy elephant?" my adversary enquires.

I shake my head.

"You have now," he whispers, leaning forward and cornering my King.

There is an awkward moment when I offer my hand for a shaking but this soon passes.

"Bedtime for us both," he says as he returns to his picture frame boudoir.

        I am asleep within seconds.
        And this magical world
            turns.

9. Play and Munch

They call me Toby. It seems to please them. And that's OK. They seem to need pleasing, these people. If just me doing what I do does the job, then well, it's a Buddha life. A Buddha life it is. They call this place a sanctuary. Sepilok Orang-utan Sanctuary. I guess it is in a way. Perhaps I take it for granted, feeding time, the photographs and the rest. But then you take what you can get these days. I didn't ask to be cute. And ginger. Certainly not ginger. If you're going to describe my colour, well I prefer reddish brown to brownish orange. Just a matter of personal taste.

By all accounts, I'm something of a celebrity around these parts. People I have never met before call my name and take photographs of me. My two best friends, Gerald and Caspian try to get in on the act sometimes by bumming each other. The people taking photographs think one is a male and one a female. If only they knew. Gerald and Caspian aren't even gay. What some Orangutans will do for publicity. They really do us no favours at all. As insecure as those Pandas they have in China.

I went out with a Panda once. Well, it was a one night stand really. She wrote to me twice. Very clingy. I recall singing her that Bob Dylan song "Just Like a Woman" and replacing the word *woman* with the word *panda*. I thought it was hilarious at the time. She cried. Just like a Panda. Gerald and Caspian were wetting themselves when I told them. Literally.

You may have heard the term 'criminal mastermind'? Well I am what is called a 'mischieval mastermind'. I create mischief and I'm getting better at it all the time.

A week ago I wrote to the President of France offering him a solution to the housing market crisis. I am yet to receive a reply. Trees are where it's at, man. Trees are where it's at.

Sometimes you have to wonder just who evolved from whom. My mother once told me that the secret of life is the space and distance between one heartbeat and the next. I have no idea what she meant by that. Perhaps I never will. But that doesn't mean I have to convince everyone else she was right. Maybe that's the difference between us animals and humans. Have a laugh. Move on. It's a big sky day and the curtain is about to open.

Showtime!

***

On entering the Sepilok Rehabilitation Centre, Faz leads me to a prefab in which I and several others are shown a film about the history of the Centre and its continuing work. I learn the following:

- Sepilok Orang-utan Rehabilitation Centre was founded in 1964, to rehabilitate orphan Orang-utans.
- The site is 43 sq km of protected land at the edge of Kabili Sepilok Forest Reserve.
- 60 to 80 Orang-utans are living free in the reserve.
- 25 young orphaned Orang-utans are housed in the nurseries.
- The facility provides medical care for orphaned and confiscated Orang-utans as well as dozens of other wildlife species.
- Some of the other animals which have been treated at the centre include: Sun Bears, Gibbons, Sumatran Rhinos and the occasional injured elephant.

Sitting in that room surrounded by strangers and watching a DVD when just hours ago I was walking through the blackness of the jungle with just the eyes of a Western Tarsier to guide me, well that's something of a thing to get your head around. It's like I've turned the pages of a picture book from Medieval Castle to Science Lab. Phew. Sometimes this life is more than I can take.

It's like when I moved from the city of Chelmsford to the little village of Tollesbury. Within days I found myself gazing upon brighter stars and revelling in quieter times, unable to comprehend how I had ever felt halfway content in any other setting but Tollesburyville.

As the bright morning Borneo sun yellows up the day, so I long for the liquorice black of a thick jungle night.

Ostensibly I've come here to watch the feeding of the Orang-utans. I follow the signs, clomping across wooden bridges and platforms, people in front and people behind, all clomping and shuffling, clicking their cameras and flicking tiny insects from the periphery of their vision.

"I'll leave you here," says Faz to me. "Meet us back at the van when you're ready."

I nod and smile a farewell to my friend. Though he is gone, I know he watches over me still.

The conservation jungle magic is all around me but I have somehow bordered my vision with black plastic strips. For I'm not in the midst of it now. I'm watching a TV somehow somewhere, feet up and beer in hand. Perhaps it was the cinema feel of the intro video that sparked this malaise. Who knows? Who cares? Just press play and munch, boys. Just press play and munch.

              So here we are
              (deep breath)
        in the depths of the jungle
                oooh.

In front of me as I lean upon the grey wooden fence is about the thickest trunkest tree I've ever seen. Halfway up, conveniently at eye-line, there is a square platform that juts out all the way around. In the far left hand corner is a crouchy man, disgruntled and bothered. He looks like he'd like to be anywhere but here. He's just waiting, waiting for I don't know what. I wonder how he got this job, whether he was once interviewed and on being successfully appointed did he just hang his head or shriek in joy and drink in joy but somehow lost all that joy along the way? Through the cracks in the planks upon which I stand. Just lost it. Along the way? Or is he on community service for a crime he did so fully commit? No idea. You make this look so easy, David Attenborough. It's a knack, I'll give you that. A kackedy-knack.

And here they come
here they come
here.
they
come
those cheeky Macaques!

It doesn't take me long to realise that this feeding platform has been set up for the three Orang-utans who lounge up on the tree in the top right hand corner of my vision. One is leaning back serene sublime and the other two are, well, they seem to be flirting in a rather uncomfortable way. But in the foreground, just a few metres from me, there's a little grey monkey with bright orange eyes, a snifty black nose, tufty white ears and a mischief aura that all but knocks me over. And he has a long old tail all black and white stripy stripe that seems to me to be nothing more than an alibi. He creeps up one of the struts of the platform, turns to the crowd and places a little finger to his little mouth whilst winking. Then in a single motion he leaps onto the platform and whisks away a piece of fruit. Magical thief oh magical thief!

Ladies and gentlemen of the jury.

Wish, swish.

Cleared.

Not guilty and steppedy step up the road to further adventures of fun and frolic!

You pesky Macaque!

And across the rope swing the Orang-utans, orangy rust swing and sway, swing and sway, landing on the platform with a thud, thud, thud, before sitting down for their tasty fare. Oh where oh where can there be a sight such as this? Chomping and chomping, spraying juice all loose and lush as I watch grinning. Just grinning.

But what's this? That pesky Macaque is back! He is shinning up the strut and poking his head above the wooden parapet. He reaches out a tender arm and clasps what looks like a peach. It's just within reach, but so is he from one of the elongated arms of an Orang-utan. He leaps at the last moment and disappears into the jungle with his fleshy prize, leaving the serviette handed to him by his big red friend to flutter by in the air towards the very edges of my flutterby dreams.

The rest of the meal passes high up in silence and when they are done, the satiated Orang-utans lollop back into the trees.

Faz taps me on the shoulder and I turn.

"Are you ready to go now? The Proboscis Monkey sanctuary is next. It's only a few minutes' drive away."

I nod and follow Faz to the waiting bus. When we arrive, Cheng is tapping away on his laptop. The moment he sees us, he flips down the lid and stores the laptop beside him in a single motion.

"Dutch Monkeys?" he enquires, catching my eye in his rear view mirror.

I smile. How could I not?

"Yep. Dutch Monkeys."

And he skid roars the three of us out of the car park and back onto the crumbling road.

When we arrive at the Proboscis Sanctuary, it is Faz this time who remains in the bus. Cheng leaps out grinning and bids me do the same with a beckoning movement of his hand that seems just like he is trying to catch and consume air.

Once back outside, I feel the intensity of the heat, a heat intensified by the lack of Faz's shadow I think. Nodding farewell to him as I follow Cheng's rapid, bow-legged gait, I feel uncertain, apprehensive.

The heat burns on

The heat burns

on

More wooden platforms, up some broad wooden steps to a higher platform and here we are, myself and Cheng, looking into the trees that surround us, picnic tables just the other side of the wooden fence that encloses the platform we are on. Unlike the Orang-utan sanctuary, it feels that we are now in the domain of the animals. And Faz is not with me. I so wish he was.

There is a rustling of leaves and then a thud, yet I see nothing. More rustling and more thudding – doomph, doomph, doomph. Cheng stands still.

"Don't move," he says. "They come."

And come they do.

From the left and the right and the middle they emerged from the backdrop like sinister revellers who have been out all night, blinking into the sun, unshaven and ready to go at it all over again. There are big ones, small ones and in-between ones, grouping in what seems like families around the various picnic tables upon which I see now (how I missed them before, I have no idea) are various small fruits similar to those I had just seen pilfered by that cheeky Macaque.

It is as I am surveying this scene that the boards upon which Cheng and I stand begin to tremble. And they tremble some more. There's a boom that begins and a boom that follows –

louder and louder
tremble and tremble
tremble and tremble me
boomer and boomer
shudder and shake
shudder and shake
me

As I courage myself up to turn around, a fully grown Proboscis Monkey leaps past my left shoulder, clears the wooden barrier upon which I have been leaning and lands with no grace at all upon the earth, scattering twigs and rotten fruit to all corners of this place. His friends and family watch on. He joins the table back and to the left of me and his fellow monkeys – of whom he is clearly the largest – shuffle over to make room. Brushing a leaf from his stomach, he slaps the table with one of his hands and at once the meal begins.

There is none of the languid munching exhibited by the Orang-utans and certainly the cheeky Macaques (if there are any about) keep their cheeky distance. For this is not a time for cheekiness. There is a dignity here, an order and a serenity that touches me. I count seventeen Proboscis Monkeys around the three picnic tables, all gently chewing the fruit and passing it to one another – all in silence, all in reverence.

"Amazing," I say aloud.

"You see me wife tomorrow," Cheng replies. "She amazing."

I smile and look over to him, but he is as lost in this scene as I. Were his round spectacles not so gleaming in the Borneo sun, I believe I would detect a Borneo tear.

The monkeys finish their meal, one by one leaving their respective tables when they are full and congregate in small groups, maybe to discuss the quality of the food, global warming or the how it ever came to be that Homo sapiens were ever graded above them in the evolutionary scale. Nothing is beyond these wonderful peoplemonkeys, nothing. It is as I am musing upon the manipulation of history that I look up towards the nearest tree. And what I see stops my heart. Entirely.

A baby Proboscis is tumbling through the air, its mother's arms outstretched, her small eyes wide and her floppy red nose swinging in ABSOLUTE agony. It is seconds before the tiny monkey hits the ground yet it seems like my whole life time. Suddenly there is a mass scurry and thump and throb as all the other Proboscis charge towards the fallen one. I turn away. From peace to barbarous animals within seconds. There is no way I want to see this beautiful creature ripped limb from limb. I thought the meal was over.

But something makes me turn back. Perhaps it is love. Yes it must be love, love, love. I turn to see the biggest of the Proboscis Monkeys, the one who had leapt over my left shoulder, cradling the baby in his muscular grey arms, holding it to his huge belly, leaning down, his rubber red nose softly stroking the baby's head. The mother thuds down and takes her baby from this hero of mine. Now it is not just Cheng who has a tear in his eye, but I.

A tear.

I.

I follow Cheng in silent elation back to the van. He is rolling, bowling ahead of me and there is no way I can keep up – not in this heat, not with my heart having grown so very, very big, swollen by salty tears and primitive prime emotion.

Ooh, ooh the funky human.

Once back in the van it seems to me that Faz has been in some kind of slumber. He has a curious smile upon his face and his eyes blink at me as if to confirm I am really real. It seems that Cheng is now in charge. The power with which we roar away gives me no doubt.

The final words I hear from Faz for the next hour are:

"Turtle Island."

I barely have time to receive them before I am thrown back in my seat.

For Cheng is on a mission.

We are heading for a boat moored at Sandakan harbour and it seems we have a schedule to keep for the trees and the roadside shacks fall away like they never existed at all. I am bumped all over. The sweat upon Cheng's face drops backwards towards me and Faz just sleeps through it all. At one point I swear the land has exchanged places with the sky, that the jungle trees have become part of the van and the battered road nothing but a piece of string that yanks us along to our destination.

I somehow see the lower streets of the downward slopes of Sandakan lined with cheering and clapping barefooted souls, roaring us on, the market emptied to swell the throng. Even the woman who I saw asleep amongst the fish has roused herself, whistling with the best of them before falling asleep once again. My trainer sales lady friends blow kisses towards me but such is Cheng's speed I have no time to respond.

On two wheels we sideslide down towards the harbour. Still Faz sleeps. I am invigorated beyond belief.

Cheng handbrakes to a stop and minutes later I am sitting in a ten foot boat with the Buddhas of Borneo. A dwarf in full sailor regalia guns the engine and we are on our way towards Turtle Island and to ecstasy.

10. Starlove

Oh starlove
starlove
my love
oh yeah...
it's only starlove that holds us all
only
starlove
well
that's all I know
and
most of the time
I'm not afraid of
starlove
anymore
honest.

But there are no stars yet. None that this fool can see anyhow. But his eyes are ever-widening.

As the dwarf captain guides the boat from where it has been moored, I feel the gentle bounce of the waves wash through me though they splashsplosh only the hull. We are all one – the dwarf captain, Faz, Cheng, the boat and I. It's like I suddenly have a multitude of hearts throbbing and pulsing, guiding me through this strange, strange life of mine.

I've never been on a boat this small so far out to sea but I know now that I will love them, like so many other marvels, forever. Soon I dismiss any thoughts of how all this works and just accept that it does. That permits me to look ahead and around at this horizon wonder that almost tips me into the sea itself.

>Oh man oh dwarf oh man oh lover
>that's us
>that's it
>sailing upon the South China Seas.

I look behind me as the land recedes and Sandakan diminishes. The hills that envelope it, invisible from foot or road now rise into my vision fully formed and dominant. They seem to grow larger as we move away from them instead of smaller, not following us but rising above us, rocking and rolling, rolling and rocking, extending into the highway of the skyway.

As I look to my right I see hundreds of houses on stilts standing proud of the water. At first glance it is like there has been a lemming jump of multi-coloured cars into the sea all jumbled and close and shook up. But as we get nearer I see the doors and the windows, the wooden planks and the stilts. And I realise it is the water village that I could see from up by the Buddhist temple.

"That's where I live," says Faz above the roar of the motor. "Over there. In the water village."

I think of him watching the Liverpool games with his friends amidst the tin of the house and the schlap of the water against the struts, intent upon every pass and every movement. I wonder if he watches football the way I have been watching the wonderful wildlife of this wonderful land – does Liverpool away to Southampton hold such wonder for him?

And I find in that moment Faz is elevated above all – certainly above the dwarf captain who gazes ever forward. He's a tiny little bastard. But he's our captain all the same. And a captain is a captain forever. I wonder how Turtle Island can surpass how I am feeling right now.

Buddhas to the left of me
Buddhas to the right
here I am
stuck in the middle
with love.

As the coastline subsides so three islands ease from the seas and into my vision. They begin as dots and emerge as land. Our dwarf captain keeps his course straight and in time I see the edges of Turtle Island before me. Cheng is on his feet at the rear of the boat. The dwarf captain turns, frowns and barks an order. Cheng sits begrudgingly but his grin just gets wider. He whips out his laptop, types like a maniac and then flips it away again. The dwarf captain shakes his head and slows down the motor, allowing our boat to drift towards the pale yellow shoreline.

We are still some yards away from the sand when the dwarf captain declares that our time aboard is up. I look at Faz who nods and steps out knee deep into the sea. I follow him and Cheng, well, he remains where he is, I guess not wanting to get his laptop wet.

I can see my English feet through this magical water. And around them are fish that should be in The Louvre so beautiful are they, so gorgeous are they, so elusive are they. I move and they groove. I groove and they back off instantly in a spasm of colour and wriggle – like many a perturbed woman has done so many times before. I reach the beach and squelch my toes into the soft squelch sand, and just stand there with the sea behind me, the blue sky above and Turtle Island before me. Were it not for Faz calling my name I may still be standing on that beach to this day.

The dwarf captain and Cheng drag the boat out of the water and follow Faz and me up the beach to where the trees extend across our vision. On the other side of the trees, to the right, is a wooden building into which Faz disappears. He returns moments later with a set of keys for each of us.

"Follow me," says Faz. "I'll show you where the rooms are."

The heat is so hot now, so naked and so virulent.

As we walk past the reception building, I see a low fence to my left that serves to enclose hundreds of small green netted tubes that poke out of the sand, maybe a foot high and just a little less in diameter. There are row upon row of them. I stop and stare.

"That's the hatchery," says Faz. "Where the turtle eggs are buried."

"Wow," I say. "There's loads of them."

"There needs to be," he replies. "Not many make it."

I gaze for a while at the sandy surface and try to imagine the tiny turtle babies in their eggs beneath the sand. It fills me with a sudden sadness, an overwhelming sense of helplessness.

By the time I have averted my eyes, Faz, Cheng and the dwarf captain are yards ahead of me. I walk towards them and they wait.

"What do you think of that?" Faz asks, pointing to his right through a gap amongst a small huddle cuddle of bushes.

I follow where he points and see a rudimentary five-a-side football pitch. I can only see one ragged goal leaning drunkenly out of the sand but it is sufficient to thrill me.

"Blimey. A football pitch out here."

"Drop your things in your room and I'll meet you here for a game," says Faz.

It feels as if he has just asked me to marry him. Of course I say yes.

Now it is me that moves on ahead, a stone building thirty yards or so in front. I hold my key before me as if it is a torch and I am in complete blackness. It leads me on and guides me to a door that opens out into a stone lobby that has four doors leading off it, behind which are a room each for me and my mad crew. I don't even explore my room, just pull on my old Dagenham & Redbridge shirt before hurling my canvas bag into the humming and return back out like I did when I was nine years old, having rushed my dinner and tumbled out the door to meet my little friends over the park for a game of Wembley Knockout.

When I get to the pitch, Faz is already awaiting me. He has taken up his position between the goalposts, resplendent in a yellow 1980s Liverpool away shirt. There is what looks like a ball fifteen yards in front of him. *Just inside the area*, I think to myself. I pick it up and move it further to the left so I can add a bit of curl. It's the strangest feeling football I have ever held. It seems to move ahead of me, becoming egg shaped yet when I stand still and hold it, it's clearly round.

The sun bears down to take a peek at these lads and I place the ball in a decent spot – one that is not covered in stones and fallen leaves.

"Ready?" I call to Faz, grinning oh grinning.

Faz nods his head, too cool to speak, his legs spread, his feet pawing at the stand and his smiling face staring straight back at me.

"Get ready to pick out of the net!"

"There is no net."

"Details, details."

I take a few steps back, breathe deep like Beckham and strike a right footed curler towards the top far corner of the leaning goal.

The ball soars through the air and curls just at the last moment, but Faz, he leaps to his left and not only gets to it but plucks it two-handed out of the sky. I do declare it moved towards him at the last moment.

Whilst I'm bemoaning my luck, my head bowed, all Pearced and Waddled, I sense a movement ahead of me. Faz is holding the ball before him. I watch as he closes his eyes and exhales gently.

No teary Gascoigne I, for the ball I have just seen saved slowly falls apart as a million or more butterflies float into the air, above the trees, into the blueness of the skyness to Nirvanaville.

"That's incredible," I say when I can finally speak.

"It's just life," Faz says. "That's all. Just life."

And instantly I see that he is right.

It is just life.

Wow.

I follow the butterflies through the trees to the beach and splash around in the sea for a while, making true friends of the fishes whilst alternately lying on the sand and staring at the sun. I once had someone say to me that he spent years staring at the sun in Regent's Park and nothing happened – that he did it for an afternoon in Chelmsford and he was detained under the Mental Health Act. He would have loved those butterflies.

As the sun sets so I return to my room. Faz has advised me to get some sleep because all the action will happen in the early hours of the morning – for that is when the Giant Turtles leave the sea and give birth on the beach.

It seems I have barely closed my eyes before I hear a knocking on the door. I rise precariously, open the door and blink wildly for Faz has a torch in his hand.

"It's time," he says. "It's time."

And time it is.

Were it not for the light of Faz's torch, we would both be hemmed in by complete blackness. I can hear my heart drum rock n roll and I bloody love it. I glint a glint of a goalpost and blow a kiss to the sky. Moments later, we are on the beach and are greeted by the sea gush of wave slop as the water flows back and forth up the shoreline. There is another torch light to our left, far down at the edge of the sea.

"Cheng is waiting," Faz says.

"What for?"

"You'll see."

"Where's the dwarf captain?"

"He never existed."

"Really?"

"Who knows?"

Not I.

Not I.

Faz turns off his torch as does Cheng. The air is still and the stars are starbright. The only external sound is the sound of the South China Seas.

Yet what is this I hear on this mad Borneo night, this mad universe night?

It's a breaking of the breaking of the waves. The splosh has turned to a sploosh and the seas are emptying.

When I see the shadows crawl from the waters, I think of the Normandy landings and of the Prisoners of War in the Sandakan Camp. I think of Gunner Owen Campbell, Bombardier Richard Braithwaite, Private Nelson Short, Warrant Officer William Sticpewich, of Private Keith

Botterill and Lance Bombardier William Moxham – the sole survivors of the Sandakan Death Marches. And I think of my grandad, that lovely man who made me and my brother a wooden fort with his own hands – hands that once held a gun, hands that once held the hands of my beautiful nan on their wedding day so long ago. It's all coming home to me now.

But it's not soldiers, weary or otherwise, who are one by one emerging from the sea, but Giant Turtles. I see them in silhouette as they sidewaddle out into the starlight, the grace of their underwater beauty replaced by an awkward attempt to walk with decorum. But they have not come here to impress the likes of me – these are mother turtles who having swum for thousands of miles have reached the shores of this island to give birth to their young on the beach before me.

> They are the dark tears of the ocean
> and I am so very small;
> the teardrops of the ocean
> and me
> so
> small.

"Watch," Faz whispers to me. "But don't move."

By this point I am able to count thirty-four Giant Turtles on the beach, all arrayed as if they have fallen from the black night sky. For a moment there is silence and then, as one, they begin to dig. Their huge rear fins paddle in the sand, digging and digging down, down, deeper on down. It's as if a thousand violins have just struck up in an orchestra pit, digging in unison, deeper on down.

"That's for the eggs," Faz tells me.

I nod. Well I think I do. It's so hard to tell.

The holes get deeper and the stars shine brighter. My heart beats faster and Cheng watches ever more keenly out to sea, observing each wave that comes in and sighing as they recede back into the darkness.

As the digging stops so a hum thrums in the air.

"They don't even know we're here now," says Faz. "We could walk right up to them and they wouldn't move. They give birth in a trance."

It is then that I notice several other men to the right hand side of us – all dressed in khaki shorts and green t-shirts. The men divide themselves up amongst the Giant Turtles and wait by each hole, a bucket at their feet.

"What…"

"It's OK. It's how they do it. It's conservation. They are rangers."

One of the Giant Turtles is just a few feet from me. I gaze enraptured as one by one, white ping-pong shaped eggs roll into the hole from the depths of the mother. One after another, sister after brother. No sooner has the egg hit the damp sand than the ranger watching on, crouching down, removes it and places it gently into his bucket. Ten, twenty, thirty, forty and more eggs from that one magnificent creature yet the hole that she now covers with the very flippers that created it is filled with nothing but sand.

"She doesn't know," says Faz as I look across at him. "The ranger will take them now to the hatchery where they'll bury them under the green net tubes."

I stare after the mother as she makes her way back into the sea, joined at intervals by all the other turtles who have laid so many eggs and filled so many empty holes. As soon as their front flippers touch water, they are away, floating in ecstasy for a while before slipping back relieved and unburdened into the ocean.

The beach is clear. It's like none of it ever happened.

But Cheng, he still stands where he has stood all along, his torch now back out and shining, waiting, waiting, waiting.

"Is he alright?" I ask Faz.

Faz nods.

"He just misses her, that's all," he replies.

"Misses who?"

"Her," he says and points to the area of sea a few yards ahead of where Cheng stands.

There is a bulge in the shorebound wave and I see it is another Giant Turtle but one much larger than those that have since disappeared back into the sea. And unlike those, this one, on making the beach, stands upon its rear flippers, stands full and tall, not a totter or wobble, just magnificent. Cheng can't take his eyes off her.

"Cheng's wife," Faz tells me.

I furrowbrow a look at him, wide-eyed and curious.

"His wife?"

Faz nods.

"They love each other very much."

"But how do they communicate?"

"Email. Probably," he replies.

There is nothing I can say, nothing I can do but turn back to where Cheng and his Giant Turtle wife are standing beneath the brightening stars. And then slowly, ever so slowly, Cheng reaches out and gently holds his wife's front flippers. I can see her big eyes from here. I am in awe. My mad driver Cheng. Oh yeah.

And

they

dance.

It's a twirl and a whirl in the swirl of the scene with the South China Seas flowing like a deep blue dress as a breeze eases through the trees that anchor this whole crazy Turtle Island to this earth of mine. My ears are full of chime and tingle. My heart has stopped beating for I no longer require it as I watch Cheng and his wife turn in circles in the sand. The more they turn, the more I notice that they are floating now, floating and turning above the beach. All is weightless. The stars lend them their sparkle and the stars fade as this bright shiny couple show me love, show me starlove. Oh starlove.

The Dharma Wheel

turns

I close my eyes

tight

and

in a spinkle

I am

gone…

(the end)

Other Books by Stuart Ayris

Novels:

FRUGALITY Book 1: Tollesbury Time Forever
FRUGALITY Book 2: The Bird That Nobody Sees
FRUGALITY Book 3: I Woke Up This Morning

A Cleansing of Souls

Poetry:

Bighugs, Love and Beer

If you could possibly take the time to leave a review on Amazon, that would be really wonderful!

A huge thank you to Kath!

And here's my email address if you ever want to get in touch: stuartayris00@gmail.com

Cheers
Take care
Stu

Lightning Source UK Ltd.
Milton Keynes UK
UKHW040628251119
354195UK00003B/628/P